STARSEED FLUX

STARSEED FLUX

Book One
of the
Starseed Chronicles

Stephen Lloyd Webber

TMMW LLC

CONTENTS

THE WEIGHT OF WAITING

In which I count stars alone, get stood up by Tam, and call my best friend for support, unaware that the universe has other plans.

My name's Mott Fortress.

Yeah, "Fortress." The last name maybe gives you the impression that I'm cooler than I really am. The truth is, I don't really stand out from the thousands of others aboard the IHC-111.

I work in maintenance. Everyone here has a job that was decided for them before they were born. Like all the others, I will spend my entire life crewing these ships. I was born a part of this fleet, and I'll die that way. It wasn't my choice to be a seeder, but if all the training programs I've watched over the years have conditioned me to believe anything, it's that all of us aboard the IHC-111 are being brought up and trained to contribute to an important mission. The future of humanity may depend on our success. So, along with all the others, I toe the line. On weekdays, at least.

I stood at the observatory deck in my dark blue IHC uniform, the fabric worn soft at the elbows from long hours bent over machinery. The deck was my favorite place on the ship—a vast chamber with a ceiling that arched upward in a high peaked roof of diamondglass panes that offered an unobstructed view of the cosmos. The deck was refreshingly empty today, the usual buzz of crew members replaced by the near-perfect silence of environmental systems and the occasional ping from the sector navigation display.

My eyes fixed out beyond the transparent pane on the void of space. I was counting the stars—or trying to, anyway. It's a game that my boyfriend Tam and I have: keep your eyes fixed straight ahead and try to count the total number of stars in your field of vision. The game had started on one of our first dates, when I'd confessed that my sensitivity to picking up other people's emotions sometimes made it hard for me to know what I was feeling myself, and in those moments I needed to decompress by staring out at space. He seemed touched by me mentioning this, and suggested we head here, to the observation deck, to see how fully we could decompress in each other's presence. And before long, it became our simple, secret way of enjoying the warmth of each other's presence against the backdrop of outer space's far reaches.

It was an impossible game. There are far too many stars and nebula to count, but I loved to try, to just stand and take it all in, make my field of vision as broad as it could be and estimate the tens of thousands. Or rather, try to stretch the sharp clarity at the center of my vision so that it expanded wide enough to take in every distinct star, the shape and size and color and the unconstellated proportions between each and every dot against the rich pure black of space. From this vantage point, I could see the great spiral arm of our galaxy stretching across the view like a river of light, punctuated by patches of cosmic dust that created dark rifts in the starfield.

Behind me, the deck's nav charts cast a soft blue glow of sector location data for all the ships in our fleet, stellar cartography, and the measurements that helped keep our vessel on its journey. The screens tracked our current position relative to nearby stellar bodies, including asteroid Bx5-1a2-Micro, which hung like a misshapen pearl against the black.

I was expecting Tam to swing by any minute now in his custom Spaceracer. His was one of the sleekest models of junkcraft anyone was ever likely to see. Junkcraft was the only kind of vehicle officially allowed for any of us on the IHC until we graduated. To have one, you had to make your own piecemeal from scrap off the mothership or one of the mining ops. Sure, it's a ship made from scrap, but it's something to call your own. The fact that Tam had incrementally and painstakingly built his to such a high degree of aesthetic expression showed how much care he could put into something he loved.

I had big plans for the two of us to have a quiet romantic day together. It was the weekend, and that meant some much-needed rec away from chores and study. I wanted the two of us to have a little getaway on asteroid Bx5-1a2-Micro, a small celestial body that for the next few weeks would still be near enough to our ship that we could travel to it.

Bx5 was riddled with peculiar energetic emanations that rose from columns somewhere deep within the asteroid's core. A subtle multicolored glow, nothing overwhelming on the physical material plane, but unmistakably present at a subtle energetic level. People claimed that spending time bathing in these emanations would be therapeutically analogous to ancient human hot springs, which apparently was something people had done on Earth. As for me, I just thought the idea sounded romantic. Escaping there would be a getaway just for the two of us, away from the familiar interiors of IHC-111 and the hums of machinery which had become the soundtrack of my work life, always reminding me of components that needed fixing.

As if on cue, the nav chart pinged. I glanced over. Faulty sensor relay in the H sector. I ignored it. On recdays, someone else's problem is actually someone else's problem.

My comm channel buzzed. Seeing it was Tam, I opened the signal flow. Tam's holograph popped in front of me, his emerald eyes a bit dewy, maybe, or pained—was that regret I saw in them? The very last expression I wanted to see today.

I should probably let you that picking up on emotions was basically my special ability. I usually had a good sense for whether someone had good intentions, bad ones, or—like now—whether they were about to deliver bad news. If everybody had a gift, this was mine. If everybody had a curse, this was also mine.

"You know how much I like you, Mott," he said, his voice interrupted by small bursts of static, "You're an amazing woman, and you're so special to me. It's just—my compartment AI is glitching out. If I don't debug it now, it'll wreak long-term havoc on the heating systems. You know how temperamental my Racer gets."

My fantasies of finally getting some one-on-one time with the love of my life—the connection, the shared laughter—crushed. For today, at least. So, maybe not crushed. Maybe just folded and put to the side for later.

I nodded and gave a weak smile, "Of course. Your safety comes first, Tam."

I hesitated. Was now the time for me to tell him how much he meant to me?

But his communication channel had already blinked out, the silence of the deck broken only by the occasional beeping of the ship's system.

He was busy, I concluded. Brilliant and busy. Now wasn't the time for me to bring up such serious matters. I couldn't just spring something like that. It was hardly romantic of me. A person needed to have the right setting for something like that, plus I would need to know just how to say it. What would Captain Alpha do?

Captain Alpha, of course, would write another chapter in his endless self-help manual series *Courageous Captains: How to Navigate the Treacherous Waters of Space*. Everyone knew space didn't have waters, but everyone also knew that it was just an analogy, and that being pedantic about analogies wasn't a good way to make friends.

I realized how much I needed support right now. Flicking the appropriate biodetails to my personal interface, I called my best friend Beryl and invited her over.

Let the official record show: I, Mott Fortress, maintenance worker number 3325, possessing no particular distinction beyond being occasionally useful with a wrench, did everything by the book today. I followed protocol. I accepted disappointment with grace. I sought appropriate social support through approved channels.

How the hell was I supposed to know the universe had other plans?

2

PROTOCOLS AND PROVERBS

We laughed at mission statements until we couldn't any-more. Turns out, the Maltans have a way of making you take things seriously.

Back in my personal cabin, Beryl and I devoured snacks, chugged synthmead and reminisced about all the ways we had managed to get ourselves into trouble over the years, all the times we'd had to fast-talk our way back to safety.

"We're old enough they should start letting us do what we want. We're going to be in charge of stuff eventually. It's stupid how long they make adults wait before *they* consider we've come of age."

My shoulders slumped as I sank deeper into the chair, the synthetic leather creaking beneath me. A strand of hair fell across my eyes, and I blew it away with an exasperated groan. Inside, frustration bubbled up—I felt like the older sibling to everyone else on the IHC-111. I never really got to live my life. No one trusted me with real responsibility. I had all the capability but none of the freedom.

"Logically, you do realize, the elders were once kids as well. Maybe they were rebellious too in their day."

"Those stiff prudes? This, I refuse to believe. All they care about are orders and regulations... and more orders and regulations."

Beryl was eating cracker puffs from a small pouch. She tossed one for me to catch in my mouth, but I missed it completely. The snack fell right between my cleavage and got stuck there.

"Bull's-eye!" Beryl burst out laughing.

I gave her a mock glare, then did an exaggerated shimmy. The puff tumbled down the inside of my shirt until I felt it reach my waist. I snatched it on its way out and triumphantly tossed it into my mouth with an open-mouthed crunch.

"Everything besides what was officially sanctioned by the seeders a thousand years ago, they don't let us do it."

"'Our eyes and our vessel's prows should gaze ever forward, ever onward!'" Beryl started quoting the IHC dogma, and this set off a chain reaction in me. I started spouting off more memorized dogma.

"'For many generations, we aboard the IHC-111 have journeyed in a victorious path toward new systems and potentially habitable planets, in a quest to aid the eternal destiny of humanity by seeding life.'"

"'The Eye Eych See Triple One, flagship vessel of the Intercosmic Humanity Commission's youngest generation!'"

We were both laughing in mad fits. The statements were based on facts, for all we knew. But they also aimed to convey a sense of heroism that, frankly, we could see no trace of in any corner of our everyday lives.

Several generations back, our great-great-great grandparents had for some reason signed up for this job. Hardly an ordinary one, that's for sure. Survive long enough to die in space. Breed replacement humans. Repeat until stars go cold.

The ship's crew was tasked to travel successfully to the next starsystem, where the ship would at last open its life dispersion capsules and thereby sow the seeds of future life. Over the course of thousands of years, even a category seven inhospitable environment would be transformed into one that could support and nurture the life seeds in the capsules. Eventually, the life seeds would produce human beings, who would grow up on the planet without any idea how they got there. But they'd be human, and their whole future would be shaped by what they decided to do with it.

Meanwhile, we aboard the IHC-111 and PNO-80 and BZT-7, the three ships of our fleet, would continue traveling into other systems using the life dispersion capsules in the appropriate places until the end of time, or until chance brought us at last to a system with a planet that could actually support human life as-is.

The odds of this were impossible to calculate. Alas, faster-than-light travel and stasis sleep technology were still the stuff of dreams and science fiction. Our ships were capable of impressive speeds, but even the fastest ship propulsion systems still required the rise and fall of several generations of human life before making it to other star systems.

Several generations had come before me, and several again would pass before the ship reached its intended destination. Ours was fated to be a life of memorizing dogma, adhering to rules, and staying the course. An entire human lifespan committed to a mission that preceded us and which would outlast us by centuries.

Which was preferable, I wondered? Us, following an unending generation-spanning mission from birth to death, or the humans we were seeding, who would wake up and start a new civilization, not knowing anything about who they were or why they existed? All I knew was that friendship made life worth living.

Beryl's eye caught a glimpse of the time. What began as a few minutes of joking around had lapsed into a whole hour.

"My stupid, stupid, stupid lenses," she said, shaking her head. I waited for her to continue. Eventually she did. "They've been picking up some really obnoxious interference. I made an appointment to get them tweaked. When I'm in a group of people, I end up having to rely on my proximal scanner to filter out all the noise. If they don't fix these things today, I'll probably go even more nuts than I already am. And here I am late for my appointment."

Beryl was biologically nearsighted, but rather than just correct her vision surgically, she chose to wear digital contacts—they gave her the expected eyesight improvements, plus a whole bunch of visual overlays that most people found too distracting, but Beryl really loved.

Just as Beryl got ready to leave, we were interrupted by a buzz from the holoscreen.

I flipped the switch to open the comm channel.

The holoscreen spawned the stern faces of Gelda and Lemoy Maltan, siblings in one of the chief families aboard the sister ship PNO-80. They stood there stiffly for several seconds, clad in ornate ceremonial robes no less. Clearly, the conversation was meant to be more than a simple "have a good recday."

"Glorious greetings, dear young ones. How has your recday been going for you thus far?"

I wondered if such an important family really wanted to know what was on my mind.

But before I could say anything, Lemoy continued. "Mott, listen. We need you to look after our dear youWe laughed at mission statements until we couldn't anymore. Turns out, the Maltans have a way of making you take things seriously.ng clones, Jim and Jelini, for the rest of the day. Our duties call, and they need supervision." Lemoy raised his blocky eyebrows and narrowed his eyes in a manner that I knew was intended to be righteously patronizing, but which I found hard to take seriously. Then again, it could have been the synthmead effecting me.

"Oooh, duties, eh?" Beryl whisper-joked to me off camera from the room's far end. "Because you're sooo important!"

"Yes, our duties," the elder Maltan answered. "Only for the day. We can arrange to have them brought back to their quarters late this evening."

Beryl froze, stunned that she had been overheard—but not necessarily ashamed.

"I would be happy—honored—to look after your juniors," I said, making sure to convey a serious professional demeanor.

Here, I realize I should probably mention a bit about clones, because, of course, humans on your planet reproduce the normal way, which I'm sure we don't need to go into the details of at the moment. For us seeders in the IHC fleet, part of our design imperative is that we retain the same genetic makeup as the original crew, repeated through however many generations it takes until our mission runs its ultimate course. Once a member of the crew reaches the age of 30, they clone a version of themselves. They walk into a clone booth, flip a switch, and just like that, the process begins wherein a little baby of their same genetic material gestates until it's ready to be raised by the ship's AI mothering and training programs. Humans have a wonderful way of making even reproduction a matter of bureaucratic procedure.

There's a lot more to the picture, but for now, you get the point. And you'll surely appreciate the fact that, the Maltans being one of the highest ranking families, very much a part of Captain Alpha's inner circle, they would be especially emphatic about ensuring the safety of their clones.

Which is why I spoke in my most professional tone to tell them, "I will be off to pick your clones up at once."

Just then, I heard the hiss of my cabin door opening.

"As you see, we have already taken the liberty," Lemoy Maltan smiled thinly.

There, in my cabin, suddenly stood Jim and Jelini Maltan, their faces in tight-angled expressions, the remnants of a heated disagreement. Jim, tall and lanky with a mop of unruly dark hair, wore the sky blue uniform of an IHC junior technician.

Jelini, younger and much shorter, had braided her hair into an absurdly complicated pattern that most likely defied ship regulations for "reasonable and streamlined conduct." Her uniform was impeccably neat, but she'd adorned it with small, colorful pins and patches, likely handmade.

A day of supervisory duties was the last thing I had imagined for my recday. But orders were orders, and this—the Maltans didn't need to name expressly—should be treated like an order. The senior generation, those living aboard the PNO-80, had the luxury of such things. Plus, my own family not being part of the royal circle, it was far better to stay on good terms with those who were, like the Maltans.

"Oh, and by the way, Mott," Gelda Maltan added, almost as an afterthought, "we've sent over a ship—our personal shuttle. You can use it if needed."

She struck Mott as both regal and somehow out-of-touch with the everyday, like a queen who'd wandered into the wrong dream.

"My brother assures me I'm being absurd," she continued, "but I thought, well, since we have a spare vessel, we may as well ensure it can be there to help our future generation in case the need arises. Of course, I don't need to mention it's for emergencies only—shuttles are naturally quite a nuisance to keep maintained."

The temptation of having access to a personal transport from the Maltans was not lost on me.

"Of course," I said. "I mean, you're already trusting me with your clones, what more is a shuttle, am I right?"

I could tell by the pained expression on the face of both Maltans that I'd stuck my foot right square into my mouth.

"Of course." I said again, hoping a nice, terse reiteration would clean my slate.

The Maltans seemed satisfied, said their formal thank yous, and signed off.

Beryl stood up and regarded the young clones disapprovingly.

"Why do you all need to be supervised? Is there something wrong with you?"

"Say what?" Jim raised an eyebrow.

"I just wonder why you get special treatment." Beryl gestured exaggeratedly, and swept her arms wide in a heroic struggle to encompass the entire absurdity of the situation. She tossed her head back, and her short-cropped blonde hair flipped to the side to punctuate her statement with disdain. "What about everyone else? Maybe I need special supervision."

"I think they're hoping we can learn something," Jim offered.

"Yeah, they want us to be more integrated," Jelini said. "They were planning to come here and show us around, but I guess they're busy. They're always doing important stuff." She sighed. "I hate it."

Beryl rolled her eyes. But I could tell she was jealous. With some friends, you understand even the parts of their past they won't speak of. She'd lost her elder when she was very young.

She pointed at me. "I'll comm you as soon as I can." With that, she whirled around, her scanner belts clanking against each other as she stormed toward the door. The cabin door hissed open and she was through it before the sensors had fully registered her.

And she was gone, off to her eye appointment, leaving just me and the two strange young clones in my cabin.

I gave a long, long sigh, and stared at the void of space where the screen had just been. How was I supposed to look after these two junior clones for an entire day? The Maltans had a reputation of scoring their assignees harshly. My record already suffered far too many negative marks, mostly from minor accidents piloting small spacecraft, which I was terrible at. What if I had to ferry these two overactive young ones somewhere?

Meanwhile, the young clones were already getting into trouble. Jim had gravitated towards my workbench, where his hands had already found their way onto a Pyrethan multiprocessor I'd been repairing, both as a hobby and to make some extra coin. Jelini, meanwhile, had, to my utmost dismay, produced a razorstylus from somewhere and was eyeing a blank wall panel with artistic intent.

"Jim, hands off!" I said, trying to inject some authority into my voice. "Jelini, you can't draw on that!"

Surprisingly, Jim and Jelini obeyed immediately. In fact, they stared back at me as intently as a mining drone about to lose its grip on a fresh vein of ore. I guessed they were trying to figure out what kind of authority figure I might be.

I smiled, hoping to give an imitation of one of the Maltans' stern and passably benevolent expressions. Inside, I was panicking. Why hadn't the Maltans told me what I was supposed to do with these two all day? Why hadn't they specified what time in the night they'd be picking them up? And what was the correct way to look after junior clones? Were there protocols? Educational requirments? Who could I reach out to for support if I needed help?

Seeing that the two of them remained motionless, probably awaiting some statement or command from me, I realized I was going to have to wing it.

"So," I said, clasping my hands together, "what would you two like to do today?"

Jim and Jelini exchanged a glance.

"Really?" Jelini asked warily.

I gave a pert nod.

"Could we... could we see the engine room?" Jim asked hesitantly. "I've only ever toured the crew and youth quarters." He thought for a moment. "Well, I guess I did get to go to the hospital once, too. People say that the VR simulations of the engine room are actually better than the real thing, but I don't believe them. Can we go see it? You're a maintenance tech—I bet you can get right in whenever you want."

Jelini rolled her eyes. "Boring," she muttered. "We should go to the observation deck instead, and I can sketch."

Already, I felt a headache coming on. The two of them could not be more different from each other. How was I supposed to keep them both happy and occupied for the rest of the day?

"How about this," I said, trying to sound confident. "We'll start with a quick tour of Engine Room B—just the outer areas, mind you—and then we'll head to the lower observation deck. Jim can learn a few things about the engines, and Jelini can sketch whatever her heart desires. But first, you're going to help me clean my room. We're not going anywhere until it's well-ordered. Sound fair?"

They nodded, grudgingly.

There was a saying that went, "All juniors are fated to grow into their elders," and that it's a phenomenon "inevitably resisted yet in the end simply inevitable." I could see how the two of them could, over time, turn into Lemoy and Gelda. It would happen gradually, through the strange circumstances of cellular biology. Their gestures, their tones, even their judgmental glances would somehow emerge as the two energetic young clones aged, as surely as metal in a forge slowly assumes the form dictated by its mold.

Although, maybe not. I wasn't like my elder. She was cold, efficient, brilliant at ship systems but emotionally distant, more of a tactician than an unintentional empath like me. But maybe our difference had come about because I had spent so much of my time with my mentors. It probably didn't help me that they were male and overly protective. Maybe that's why everyone accused me of being so sheltered.

It only took a few minutes to create a bit of order amidst the jumble of tools and equipment littering my cabin. The paragrammic fuses and capacitors went into the wall-mounted diagnostic cabinet. My prized collection of nano-optic calibrators and nickel-platinum sheaths found their home in the maintenance locker. The spray cleaners, micropneumatic dischargers, and tri-phase solvents all lined up neatly on the workbench. I carefully stored my rare Cobalt-60 field purifier in its special padded case. The self-digesting waste buckets and autobrooms got tucked away beneath the desk where they belonged.

The universe may tend toward disorder, but we maintenance workers, we bend it back toward order.

It wouldn't be fair to say that Jim and Jelini were happy about all this, but the more we worked together, the better all of our moods became. Our task completed, it was now time for me to honor my end of the bargain.

As we left my cabin and made our way through the ship's corridors, I actually felt emboldened. Maybe this day wouldn't be a total loss after all. Who knew? It was a chance to make a positive impression on a couple of young minds, and I might even learn something new about the ship I'd called home.

I smiled.

I didn't have a clue what I was doing, but they didn't have to know that.

3

THE MACHINERY OF DOCTRINE

In which an engine room tour goes sideways, opal paste causes strange readings, and Jelini's faith in an invisible deity becomes the least weird thing happening.

It took us exactly four minutes to reach the engine room, and in that time Jim managed to somehow open the access panels to no fewer than six different control interfaces, each time earning a stern look from me, which, if it didn't stop him permanently at least proved effective enough at getting him to cease what he was doing for the time being. Jelini trailed behind, sketching something in her datapad—probably making fun of both of us, if I had to guess.

The temporary feeling of excitement and confidence I'd felt in my cabin had faded completely. What was it about kids that made them think they should be able to do whatever they wanted, whenever they wanted?

All I'd wanted for today was to whisk myself away to freedom with Tam and dream of what life could be like on the BZT with the other adults—or more, what it might be like to steal away, just the two of us, and live as homesteaders on some remote berg in the great beyond. Looking after young clones wasn't real responsibility, and it sure as hell wasn't freedom.

It wasn't the first time I'd been tasked with looking after junior crew members, though it was certainly the first time I'd been entrusted with someone with rank like the Maltans.

It had started about a year ago when I'd been assigned to change some worn parts on the climate control system in the ship's nursery. While I was there, one of the caretaker or "mother" units broke down completely and left a group of toddlers unsupervised. I'd stepped in and began entertaining the kids with improvised stories about some of the repairs I'd just done to the ship's systems, pretending that the ship components were people I knew, and dramatizing the whole thing.

I was doing my best to be playful for their sake and keep their attention off the fact that I also needed to be knee-deep into the rear access hatch of the caretaker unit fixing the thing. I persisted until I finally got the unit to reboot, and after that point, my thanks from them was that they'd quickly forgotten about me and returned their attention to one of the holos the unit was projecting.

Word of what I had done spread, and apparently people were impressed, because soon I found myself being called upon more frequently to assist in the nursery when extra hands were needed. Of course, it wasn't a role I'd sought out or particularly enjoyed—I was much more comfortable with machinery, as I'd been trained—but I did my best, drawing on my knowledge of the ship's systems to keep the kids engaged and out of trouble.

One day, during a routine inspection, Gelda Maltan herself had visited the nursery while I was there. She'd walked in on me explaining the basics of gravity generation to a group of wide-eyed five-year-olds using a makeshift model I'd cobbled together from spare parts. She had seemed impressed, and she lauded me on my ability to relate and empathize with others. I think she'd meant it as a compliment, but it embarrassed me completely.

After that, I'd noticed a shift in how the senior crew regarded me. By that, I mean that they no longer completely ignored me. Many of them had even treated me with a modicum of respect, even though I was just a mechanic, not some budding leader or educator. I was born to be a mechanic, and I very much preferred the simplicity of working with machines, where problems had clear solutions and I knew exactly where I stood.

But some of the high-ranking families had different ideas. They began to involve me in more youth-oriented projects, accusing me of a "natural rapport" with the younger generation.

And now here I was, responsible for the clones. I couldn't help but wonder if this was some kind of test—a way for them to evaluate my potential, or just some sort of punishment only the royal could conceive of. This wetwork, this dealing with human interpersonal dynamics and nurturing their development, was not what I was trained to do.

The engine room's massive double doors slid open with a hiss. The room beyond was lit by orange perimeter lights. Beyond was a sanctuary of metal and wiring and pressurized containers and walkways of diamond plate and steel grids. Towering cylindrical chambers stretched up into darkness, and they pulsed with a blue ionic glow. The low hum of the idling engines filled the air, the myriad units cased in plasmacore sleeving. Dozens of ionic dispersal units each thrummed with magnificent capacitance.

"Welcome to the—" I started, but Jim was already rushing forward, his eyes wide with excitement.

"Is that the actual matrix core?" he asked eagerly. "I overheard my supervisor talking about those. He said they're really temperamental." He pointed to a particularly bright chamber. "And those must be the harmonic restabilizers! I've read about these, but I've never seen the real ones up close!"

I had to admit, his enthusiasm was infectious, like a disease you'd rather not catch but somehow find yourself pleased to be suffering from. "Actually, those are just the auxiliary power couplings," I corrected gently.

A sharp crack interrupted me, followed by Jelini's voice: "Oops."

We turned to find her standing by a wall-mounted control panel, looking sheepish. She gripped her datapad tightly to her chest. The panel's screen was displaying an angry red warning message.

"I didn't touch anything!" she said quickly, then gestured towards an arrangement of rotating lenses and sensors mounted to a wall panel, which I recognized to be the slipscope array. "Well... I barely touched that blue thing!"

Jim was beside himself. "Jelini, you broke it! You're always breaking everything!"

I hurried over, my heart racing. Breaking equipment in the engine room was no small matter, and the slipscope array was a very temperamental component that helped us detect and analyze gravitational distortions in space. Without it properly calibrated, our next major acceleration could be disastrous. But as I looked over the panel's readout, I was surprised to see that the warning message wasn't from damage to the unit. It was picking up some kind of anomalous energy reading.

"That's strange," I muttered. "These readings... they're not like anything I've seen before." As I issued commands on the console, I noticed a strange substance on my fingertips. Was the panel overheating or leaking something?

I tried to make sense of the bizarre data. The first possibility that jumped out—never something to be ruled out when dealing with generations-old equipment—was a malfunction in the sensor itself. Clearly, Jelini had interfered with it in some way. But the readings weren't to be dismissed. They described a microscopic singularity, impossibly stable and hovering just a few meters from the sensor array. I looked in the direction it seemed to indicate, but saw nothing.

I double-checked the calibration. As far as the machine knew, it believed it was functioning normally. Whatever Jelini had done, it had triggered something very weird.

My effort trying to decipher the readings had distracted me from Jim and Jelini's bickering, but their raised voices soon brought my attention back to them.

"You took my opal paste!" Jim accused, his face flushed with anger. "That was for my neuro-pneumatics project!" He sounded on the verge of a freakout.

Jelini shot back, "Well, I put it to better use! I used it to write a poem about Invisible Skylord Ultra."

I blinked, trying to process what I'd just heard. Opal paste?

Opal paste was a viscous, iridescent compound harvested from the metabolic secretions of crystalline parasites. It gained notoriety among fringe researchers for its supposed property of creating temporary entanglement between organic and synthetic materials when exposed to certain frequencies. Though considered industrial waste, underground experimenters prize it for its unpredictable effects in consciousness-transfer trials and neural interface modifications. Was that what I had on my fingers from working with the diagnostic panel?

And Invisible Skylord Ultra? The mythical deity? In seeder society, belief in such entities was generally viewed as an embarrassing holdover from humanity's superstitious past, something most people outgrew by adolescence. The prevailing wisdom held that centuries of space travel should have cured humanity of the need for invisible sky gods. After all, they'd traversed the heavens themselves and found only vacuum and radiation. Most seeders prided themselves on their rational, engineering-focused worldview where problems had technical solutions. To believe otherwise was seen as a failure to properly mature into the clear-headed pragmatism their mission demanded.

Jim, for example, was already one with that worldview. "Come on, Jelini! You know ISU doesn't even exist!" He waved his hand dismissively. "Only kids believe that stuff anyway."

But so what if Jelini believed in a god? Maybe it meant she had come to recognize what a poor job adults had done of *really* explaining why we're all *really* stuck out here together on these floating metal contraptions. If you give people rules instead of reasons, or reasons instead of direct experience, why mock their search for meaning?

Jelini's eyes flashed. "How dare you say he's not real just because he's invisible!" She turned to me, a downright devious look crossing her face. "Mott, did you know about Jim's Secret Scriptures of Strength?"

Jim's face went pale. "Jelini, don't you dare—"

I broke in. "Jelini, I need you to be honest with me right now and tell me what exactly you did to this wall panel."

"I mean, if we're talking about made-up things..." Jelini continued.

Jim's shoulders slumped in defeat. "Fine, fine! I'm sorry I said ISU doesn't exist. Just... please don't say anything else."

Jelini looked at me, pouting, but at this point I knew better than to take her emotions in earnest. "Jim's right. I used some of his stupid opal paste." She showed me a page from her notebook, on which was drawn a strange pale diagram that looked something like a talisman or series of runes. I was impressed she had drawn something so quickly with a simple razorstylus. "It's one of the sigils used by those of us who worship ISU. I pressed it against that glowy thing. I'm sorry, Mott. I didn't mean to break anything."

Secret scriptures? Invisible deities? What exactly had I gotten myself into with these two?

Humans need myths more than we need oxygen. Give us facts and we'll suffocate. Give us stories and we'll build cathedrals in the void.

"I'm glad you understand how big of a deal this is, Jelini."

The diagnostic panel behind me let out another series of exasperated beeps. This time, instead of trying to decipher them, I used my sleeve to wipe off the surface. Removing the opal paste caused the warnings to subside.

After a reboot, I checked to make sure the equipment wasn't still malfunctioning. Everything appeared to be working normally. Whatever Jelini had done had somehow opened a viewstream for a simulated channel, nothing more drastic than that. Still, it was clear that I would need to keep a close eye on her.

CURIOSITY'S MOMENTUM

In the engine room, surrounded by systems built to last centuries, I began to understand that some things are designed to keep you in motion without ever letting you arrive.

I looked over to see that Jim had already disappeared through the archway leading to the primary thrust chamber's auxiliary cooling manifold. I took Jelini by the arm and raced after him.

"These components—all of them, big and small—they're meant to be replaceable, aren't they?" he asked, his earlier irritation forgotten. "The whole system is built for the long haul."

"It will need to last forever, which is precisely why you need to treat everything in the engine room with respect," I confirmed, and gestured at the tangled maze of high-capacity cooling tubes that snaked from the storage capacitors. Each one pulsed with a blue glow as it bled minute amounts of excess energy into the shielded compartments. "If need be, every part can be maintained or swapped out without stopping the core systems." I stopped to check the tightness of a bolt, twisting it another quarter-turn with the autospanner I always carried with me. "If it dies, we die. If it's healthy, we're healthy."

The capacitors themselves were monstrous things—ancient ceramalloy cylinders that towered three decks high, their surfaces etched with decades of service markings and emergency patch jobs. Was it all functional? Perfectly so. But was it aesthetically pleasing? Not to most. Although, to born engineers such as myself, beauty was in the eye of the beholder.

We continued our tour. On our opposite side, coolant pipes wrapped around us. They were connected to the cramped heat exchanger room where techs in environment suits were tasked to monitor the thermal bleed. On the deck below us, visible through the floor grating, power regulation systems filled a cavernous space with a low electromagnetic hum.

Between it all wound the narrow maintenance catwalks whose grated surfaces were worn smooth by generations of boots. The lighting in the engine room at its minimal level, this being a recday after all. The dim glow cast the peripheries into shadow, and left the room a maze of dark corners. I made sure we all stuck to the well-lit path.

As we walked, and I answered more of Jim's questions about engine room layout and functionality, I noticed that Jelini, although quieter than usual after her mishap, nevertheless seemed engaged, maybe even interested. She had taken to running her hands carefully along the touch-safe outer panels and cowlings, eyes half-closed, describing her perceptions more or less to herself. "This one feels...lonely," she murmured. "But that one there, it's in resonance with its neighbors."

I tried to connect her intuitive descriptions with the engineer's reality I was familiar with. "Yeah, that's really perceptive of you, Jelini. Those are harmonic stabilizers for the communication relays. Their whole job is to sync with their neighbors."

When she gave Jim a smug smile, I saw how important it was for these two to feel that they had me on their side—or at least as an ally. To them, they probably weren't sure whether I was a grown-up, and therefore unrelatable, or else a kid like them.

Although I had definitely passed into the age of adulthood, I was not yet of age to become a part of the world of grown-ups aboard the BZT, the Beltzone Trawler. For the time being, I decided that what was most important was that I kept the two of them guessing. Although, it was frustrating to be treated like a kid. Why couldn't anyone see that I was ready for real responsibility?

My mentor's words came back to me, the time when he had talked about the second-stage adulthood ceremony, the phase which marked the end of a seeder's time aboard the IHC and the start of their new career crewing the BZT: "The ancients on Earth had it rough—they had to guess when childhood ended and adulthood began. The more modern their civilization became, the less they relied on ceremonies to mark important transitions. But we seeders, we've got it sorted. Your whole life mapped out in perfect thirds: thirty years learning, thirty years doing, thirty years teaching. And if anything remained after that, it was a person's own choice."

He had a gentle smile that always made the creases around his eyes deepen. I always thought it strange that facial expressions signaling joy would, over time, nevertheless wreak havoc on the skin of the face and leave behind wrinkles. But on him, they seemed dignified.

"And here's the real thing to ponder on, Mott: even with all our planning, all our ceremonies, life still surprises us. That's the true gift of being a seeder—we get to reinvent ourselves completely every few decades. The ancients were usually stuck in one role their whole lives. When someone back on earth wanted to pick a life trajectory or change careers it was this huge, dramatic thing. But us? We get to change when we move from ship to ship—maybe an engineer becomes an administrator, and later a teacher. We get to have different vocations built right into our lifecycle. Having to change shows us how none of these vocations are really who we are inside."

After the engine room tour, we found our way to the lower observation deck. It was quieter than the upper one— less trafficked, less polished, but offered an equally magnificent view of the cosmos. Unlike the architectural grandeur above, this deck had lower ceilings that could at times even make the vastness beyond seem all the more impressive.

I'd managed to grab some snack bars from a dispenser near the entrance. "Delicious Flavor Bar 4," my personal favorite, chocolaty with a satisfying salt crunch.

"Here," I said, distributing the bars. "Not exactly a gourmet meal, but it'll have to do for the likes of us." I grinned at them and they smiled back.

Jelini seemed glad to have a snack, and began devouring hers in short order. Jim took his with a quick nod of thanks. He unwrapped it neatly before breaking it into perfectly equal pieces.

Jelini at once began working on another drawing—or what she had called poetry. I watched her furrowed brow as she scribbled furiously, her entire being focused on the page with an intensity that made me wonder what visions might be flowing through her mind.

Jim caught me watching her and gave me a knowing look, leaning in to whisper, "She's been like this ever since she found those old texts in the archive. Don't worry—it goes in phases. Last month she was convinced that certain maintenance junction panels were hallowed meditation spots."

I nodded, trying to look nonchalant, though in truth I found it touching. In our regimented society, Jelini had carved out some room for herself.

Emanating from Jim I could feel a wave of protective affection for his sister tangled with genuine worry, all wrapped in a bundle of hormone-fueled awkwardness.

"Where are your elders anyway?" I asked, trying to shift the focus. "Their message made it sound urgent."

Jim shrugged. "Some kind of special assembly. They wouldn't tell us much, but Lemoy seemed..." He paused, searching for the right word. "Excited? Which is weird. He's usually about as exciting as a dead capacitor."

"They've been having lots of secret meetings lately," Jelini added without looking up from her drawing. "Ever since that probe showed up two days ago."

My heart skipped. "Probe?"

"Yeah," Jim said, his voice conspiratorial. "The elders have been in a tizzy about it. That's probably why they're meeting today."

Initially, when he'd said "probe," I thought it might be some sign of something external—maybe from some other life. But what would be the odds of that? Actually, I'd heard Fermi had calculated it. After twelve generations, it'd be about one in ten million.

But it irritated me to even entertain the notion. How can they make a formula for something when we don't yet know the probability? The only alien life we'd encountered was so far from what people called "advanced" that I suspected it was more sophisticated and subtle than we knew how to look for.

While I distracted myself with thoughts of encountering advanced alien life, Jim and Jelini had started arguing with each other again. For the moment, though, I just couldn't care enough to intervene. I stared outside the window, and before long, they'd quieted down again.

Space would forever be our surroundings, but it never ceased to amaze me. I couldn't set aside the fact that we were on a one-way course, and the stops that we made along the way we would only ever get to see once, and never again. The asteroid field stretched before us, a glittering river of dust and ice, each fragment tumbling in its own slow rotation. Beyond, stars blazed with pure fire across unimaginable distances.

"Well you two," I said finally, "time for us to head back to my cabin."

"Oh!" Jim perked up instantly. "Could we take the maintenance tunnels back? It would be a shortcut, wouldn't it?"

Something felt off—a subtle contradiction between what he said and what he seemed to want. My instincts whispered that he was trying to con me, but surely that couldn't be true?

It was a strange suggestion, but a playful one, and it posed no real risk. In fact, I had to smile at his enthusiasm— he'd clearly been paying more attention during the tour than I'd given him credit for. And there would be something appealing about seeing the familiar passages through their fresh eyes. Maybe I could learn something from their curiosity.

"Alright," I agreed, "maintenance tunnels it is."

As we crawled through the narrow spaces, ducking under pipes and stepping over conduits, I found myself appreciating our seeder life in a new way. Yes, it was regimented, but at least it was clear. We knew who we were, what was expected of us. And every few years, we got the chance to become someone new. Maybe that was freedom enough.

5

CONVERGENCE IN THE CORRIDORS

In which Eggi appears suspiciously and Jelini asks about the sky in space.

Traveling by way of the maintenance tunnels, the three of us were largely silent, and in place of the junior Maltans' bickering or my droning on about the finer points of engine hardware, I enjoyed taking in the mundane sensory information of the IHC. The air circulators' soft sighs, the engines' low hum, the subtle creaking of metal as hull support panels expanded and contracted. These sounds had been the backdrop to my entire existence, so omnipresent I usually didn't notice them. Putting myself in the shoes of these younger clones, so impressionable and curious, it all felt like a reminder of the thin barrier between us and the great unknown.

The maintenance access tunnel stretched ahead of us, a throat of steel and carbon fiber, and in its widest section it was barely wide enough for one fully-grown person to walk normally. Jim led the way, moving with an assurance I found endearing. His lead gradually increased until eventually he was a few dozen meters ahead.

A clang echoed far ahead of us in the tunnel, followed by muttered cursing. In the dim glow of the emergency lights, I made out a figure hunched over an open access panel, a wiry young man with close-cropped red hair.

"Eggi?" Jim called out. "What are you doing here?" He turned to look at me, astonished. "I had no idea he would be here, of all places." And when his expression of astonishment went on for a beat too long, I could tell he was bluffing.

Our approach startled the figure, and he banged his head on a section of chromed conduit. He spun to face us, and I recognized Eggjern Laraon—Eggi to everyone who didn't want their own name turned into a creative string of profanity. His green eyes sized up the three of us. I caught a glimpse of he and Jim whispering to each other.

I tried to listen in on their conversation, but Jelini tugged at my sleeve. "Mott, can I ask you something? It's about the unseen world." Her eyes were earnest. "If Skylord is real— and I know he is—where's the sky in space? I've been reading about ancient terrestrial humans, how they were surrounded by sky that mesmerized them. Because of gravity and how rare flying was for them, they located their heavens above them spatially, and their gods up there. So if ISU is really everywhere, do you think I'll get to meet him someday? And if so, what should I wear?"

I opened my mouth to respond, but the dynamic between Jim and Eggi was more urgent than ancient symbolism. Eggi had surreptitiously passed something to Jim—it looked like a logbook or small box. And then he quickly disappeared around the curve of the hallway.

Suspecting mischief, I jogged toward them.

"What was that about?" I asked Jim once I'd closed the distance and caught up to him.

He shrugged, far too casually. "Oh, I was just surprised to find toilet debris in the engine room," he said loudly enough that his voice would carry around the curve of the hall. "Because that's what Eggi is. Just an annoying toilet-head that won't leave me alone."

I wasn't buying it. I pushed past Jim and jogged after Eggi, and I cupped my hands to my mouth and shouted at the departing figure, "Hey! Get back here."

But as soon as I had rounded the next bend in the corridor, there stood Eggjern Laraon, nonchalantly inspecting a section of ventilation control.

"To some, compositing hybrational variance in the power routing is merely pedestrian," he said, as if to himself, as if this were a perfectly normal thing to be doing or saying in an access tunnel in close proximity to my cabin. His fingers moved over the control's key panel as he spoke, as if he wanted me to believe he was making adjustments. "Except when there's a pattern to the fluctuations that doesn't match any known fault cascade. Fascinating stuff, really. If you map the power spikes against contrasting patterns of nonstandard diagnostic heuristics..." He trailed off, finally picking up on the fact that I was not amused.

I was, however, curious about what motivated the young clone's distinctive aesthetic. He had a reputation as something of a savant analyst, though for some reason he harbored an aversion to wearing metallic accessories. While other junior residents aboard IHC-111 typically adorned themselves with jewelry crafted from exotic alloys—titanium-vanadium composites, chromium-cobalt matrices, and reclaimed platinum-iridium components sourced from asteroid mining operations—Eggi for some reason wore an abundance of organic materials: carefully curated pieces of wood, bamboo, and bits of handwoven textiles and tapestries. To put it plainly, he was likely the only person aboard IHC-111 who clad himself in a poncho. His wrists and neck displayed an impressive collection of wooden beads and gemstone pendants.

Jelini, hands on hips, gave every appearance of being the junior to Gelda Maltan, ready to dispense a scolding. "We're on a mission to accompany Mott to her cabin," she said. "ISU gave it to us three personally. And you're not supposed to be here."

I shook my head. "We're on our way to my quarters, and if you're going to join us, you'll be expected to help prepare dinner—along with the other chores."

Eggi's joy at hearing this made it seem like he was a stray dog and I'd invited him into a palace.

Now, I understood Jim's true reason for asking us to take the path through the tunnel. And while I felt deceived, honestly, I didn't much mind. So what if Jim and his friend wanted to scheme their way into spending time together? I could hardly blame them for that. Little white lies were what this station ran on, just as much as ionic cartridges and hyperspheres. If someone could look after themselves well enough to maintain close friendships and handle their own affairs, maybe that was worth more than official rules could account for. I waved them all along, and the four of us made our way back into the residential hallway and into my cabin.

6

DISTRESS ACROSS DISTANCE

In which Beryl's paranoia proves prescient, ghost ships become real, and Jim swears undying loyalty that will definitely not lead to trouble later.

Jim, Jelini, Eggi and I had barely settled into the seats in my cabin when my comm panel lit up with an incoming transmission. At first, I was afraid it would be Tam with another romantic change-of-plans note, something that would be horrendously embarrassing to receive in front of my rapt audience of young clones. But it was just Beryl.

I saw her face on the screen. The image was grainy and kept cutting out, but her agitation came through clearly enough.

"Mott, I know how everyone jokes about my anxiety and my conspiracy theories," Either she had paused, or there was a bit of transmission loss in the message. Her voice crackled with static. "But sometimes they're real. And this time, something seriously real is happening. I've narrowly escaped for the time being, but—" She glanced over her shoulder, and I noticed other faces briefly visible in the cramped space behind her. The strange faces of unwell people.

"Beryl, where are you exactly?"

She lowered her voice. "Inside the sick ward of the royal levels. Well, it may not be the sick ward in truth. More like... I think this is a prison, Mott. You have to come save me."

"We don't have prisons," I reminded her. "We're three very busy ships with clear conditioning and rules—"

"I know, I know," she cut me off. "But this is different. Trust me. I know I can be hyperbolic sometimes. Unfortunately, this is not a secure line—I can't tell you what I saw, but as crazy as it sounds, I think for now I'm the only one who..." The transmission crackled. "Please, Mott. I need safe transport back."

A louder crackle of static burst through the transmission, and Beryl's voice returned, more urgent now. "They're talking about something the seeders aren't supposed to know about." She lowered her voice further. "They caught me listening, and I escaped to this ward. It's not just a medical facility, Mott. I'm looking at equipment I've never seen before, things that shouldn't exist. A ghost ship, Mott."

Another sound cut through the static. A door opening, voices approaching.

"Please come find me. I don't know what they're planning to do with me."

I sat frozen for a moment. Ghost ship? This didn't seem like Beryl's usual drama. Usually she had something or other she was paranoid about, like the time she'd convinced herself the security intern was sending coded messages to smugglers because his light patterns were "too rhythmic," or when she'd spent three weeks certain that the unusual amount of dark matter several systems over meant that most types of light bulbs were reversing and we'd all be blind by month's end, but seldom was there anything as concrete or urgent as this. As implausible as it sounded, the fear in her voice had been real.

The lower decks of the PNO were generally synonymized as the royal levels, owing to how the elite families had gradually taken over those areas for their personal use. Most of us aboard the IHC-111 only saw the royal fleet during mandatory health screenings—or disciplinary hearings. It was a bit unusual for one of us native to the IHC to go to the PNO for a checkup, but then I supposed digital contacts were not exactly a standard choice, and she'd probably had to pay extra for her decision to do it that way rather than at the clinic aboard our ship.

And looking at the nav chart on my cabin's display, I realized the vector to reach Beryl wouldn't be direct from our current location. We'd need to take a roundabout route through some of the asteroids. On the other hand, the Maltan's personal transport raft would have the necessary clearance codes to approach and even dock at the PNO, something my own single-seater maintenance pod could never manage without first going through bureaucratic approval. The Maltans' vessel's presence would be as unremarkable as public transit. Of course, they'd probably never imagined their precious transport being used for an impromptu rescue mission by a group of young clones and a maintenance worker. But then again, who said they would have to ever know about it?

I glanced at Eggi, Jim and Jelini, unsurprised to find them both watching the exchange with intense interest and a complete lack of discretion. Something told me they were already committed to whatever came next, already seeing themselves as part of this unfolding drama. Jelini, for one, probably saw this as a message from her Skylord-whatnot.

"We need to sort this out," I said finally. "This sounds like an emergency. And, I do have permission to use the Maltan shuttle in case of an emergency," I said finally. "Beryl, you can count on us."

"I'll need to, because I may be helpless to stop whatever the hell they are planning to do," Beryl's voice crackled through the static. Behind her, I glimpsed figures in long white coats, and some sort of gleaming stainless steel apparatus being wheeled toward her. "They're saying it's just a routine scan, but Mott—" her eyes widened as she glanced over her shoulder "—There's a mysterious vessel in our midst, and I think it came from the Sigma array..." The feed distorted, her face stretching impossibly before stabilizing again. "If I don't make it out... you need to tell everyone—" The transmission cut off.

Jim's face lit up with uncontained excitement.

"Jim," I said solemnly, "can I count on you to have my back, no matter what happens out there?"

"Absolutely," he replied with such earnest sincerity that even Jelini's quick poke to his ribs couldn't diminish it.

"Jelini, I'll need your... intuition as well. Can I count on your support?"

She gave a pert nod.

My eyes turned to Eggi, and he must have seen the expression on my face signaling a clear "no." Jim and Jelini were entrusted to my care, but Eggi was just some guy who worked in analytics.

His eyes shifted back and forth, then lit up, as if he'd arrived at the answer to a long equation. "OK, granted, you barely know me," Eggi continued, speaking to my hesitation. "But think about it. We're headed out into the unknown. You need every advantage you can get."

"What exactly are you bringing to the table?" I asked.

He grinned, recognizing the opening. "I can spot patterns others miss. And," he lowered his voice, "I bet I know ways around the PNO's monitoring protocols that even you haven't thought of."

That last bit was interesting, although in truth did even less to convince me he was a reliable and trustworthy companion. I glanced at Jim, who gave a subtle nod. I could see that he trusted Eggi, even if I wasn't sure I did.

"Alright," I said finally, making my decision. "You can come. But you follow my lead, understood? One wrong move and you're out like yesterday's toast."

Eggi's face lit up, but I held up a hand to stop his celebration. "And when this is over, you and I are going to have a long talk about those so-called protocol workarounds."

He nodded solemnly, but I could see the excitement in his eyes. I pointed at Jim. "If he does anything out of line, I'll hold you personally responsible."

Jim froze for a moment, then gave a confident nod.

7

THE ART OF PLAUSIBLE STORIES

Ghost ships haunt space. They also haunt the people who see them and the people foolish enough to try rescuing their friends from whatever darkness contains them.

Beryl's trip to the PNO had started out uneventful. She sat in the uncomfortable vinyl public transport seat and watched idly as distant asteroids and ships drifted past the viewport. The synthmead she'd drank at Mott's apartment felt painful in her stomach, and it left a sour taste in her mouth. She regretted that third glass now.

Then she saw it.

A shadow in the void, massive and indistinct—easily as large as the PNO itself. Her breath caught. Her hand flew to her chest. The thing was transparent, fully present and wholly absent. A cloaked ship? Something from another dimension? Some experimental technology?

Nothing the Company built could possibly be this large without everyone knowing. And if they had built such a thing, why hide it from their own people?

She glanced around at the other passengers—dull faces, blank expressions. Did no one else see it? She leaned forward to tap the shoulder of an elderly woman seated ahead of her.

"Whuuaah?" the woman turned, her face like a wrinkled paper bag, and no more cheerful.

Beryl, words failing her, simply pointed wide-eyed toward the massive apparition hanging in space.

The woman swatted boredly in her direction and turned back around to stare vacantly forward once more. Beryl fought the urge to physically turn the woman's head. She knew her reputation—always prone to hyperbole, always finding patterns where others saw nothing. But this was different.

She looked away, then back again. The shadow remained. An immense presence that shouldn't exist.

She needed someone more grounded to confirm what she saw. Someone who would look where she pointed and acknowledge the impossible thing hanging in space. She stood up and marched to the center aisle of transport.

"Excuse me," Beryl said, addressing the entire compartment, the urgency of the situation making her voice half an octave higher. "Please, look out there."

People glanced at her, then away, their expressions flat with disinterest or irritation. She was so full of anxiety she was jumping up and down now. She pointed more insistently at the viewport, but judging from how they looked at her untamed hair and patched-up clothes, they'd already decided she wasn't worth their attention.

She stood, moving down the aisle, trying to catch someone's eye. Anyone. She hated how separate the different crews and passenger ranks could be. Not one person gave her the benefit of the doubt and looked out the viewport where she was gesturing. It all made her feel crazy, even though she could see the revelation right there with her waking eyes. If her theory was right, nothing would ever be the same. If she was wrong... but she wasn't wrong. She couldn't be.

She turned to face the ghost ship one last time. Where had it gone?

The shuttle lurched slightly as it began its final approach. Through the viewport, the massive white hull of the PNO loomed larger.

The docking bay opened to receive them. Mechanical arms extended to guide the shuttle home.

Beryl sank back into her seat, alone and furious.

THE VENEER OF PROTOCOL

Getting past security requires two things: a plausible story and the confidence that you belong exactly where you shouldn't be.

Our walk to the shuttle bay stretched longer than usual. Every step that echoed off the curved walls of the corridor brought us closer to a destination I was less and less sure about the closer we came. The standard lighting panels cast their usual soft glow, but now every shadow prodded my subconscious about taking these young clones on an unauthorized mission.

I found myself hyper-aware of their footsteps behind me, of the small unselfconscious scrapes and shuffles of their boot soles against the hexgrate floor plates. Jim had fallen unusually quiet after his declaration of fealty, which made me concerned. People with a strong desire to be brave—or even to simply be regarded as brave—were apt to get into the worst kind of trouble.

On the other hand, there was Jelini, who I could hear humming something cheery under her breath. And then there was Eggi, the last-minute tagalong who had been suspiciously mucking around in the access corridor and later bragged about his ability to circumvent monitoring protocols. It was obvious now that he'd had a prior arrangement to meet up with Jim, but he would no doubt be getting more than he bargained for thanks to Beryl's need of a rescue. Beryl had a way of finding herself in strange situations, and this time it did seem genuinely concerning.

I shrugged my shoulders to feign a carefree attitude. I was performing the physical actions of a confident person so that eventually the rest of me could catch up to what I was directing my physical self to do.

A group of off-duty workers wearing dull red coveralls passed us, their suits stained with hydraulic fluid. Did their conversations drop to murmurs as they passed our odd little procession because they suspected something? Or was it merely a normal lull in a normal conversation, and I was overreacting? I gave them a casual nod, as if to say, "Ah, this again. You know how it is. Nothing interesting happening here."

In situations like this, the advice from Captain Alpha's self-improvement handbook, "Courageous Captains: Seven Steps to Stellar Leadership," was to keep your mind on something else—a vivid memory, something completely unrelated to the cold sweat trickling down my spine or the nagging voice in my head screaming about how I'd be scrubbing waste recyclers for the next decade if anyone questioned why I was leading the Maltans' precious clones toward the shuttle bay instead of keeping them safely occupied in the residential ward with educational holos.

"Mott," Jelini whispered, closing the distance between us once the workers had passed, "I've been thinking about the harmonics in the engine room..." She trailed off, then continued with unusual hesitation. "Do you think maybe that's how ISU communicates? Through the vibrations in things?"

Before I could formulate a response, Jim cut in. "Everything vibrates. That's just basic physics."

"Exactly!" Jelini's voice rose with excitement. "So that proves he's everywhere."

I heard footsteps ahead.

"Shhhh," I cautioned. We were approaching the first security checkpoint before the shuttle bay. I pulled them both into a maintenance alcove, my mind racing. I hadn't thought this far ahead. How exactly was I planning to explain this to security?

I also realized I'd left my autowrench back in my room. Hopefully I wouldn't need it.

"Listen," I whispered, "when we get to the checkpoint, let me do the talking. Whatever happens, try to act... normal. Don't say anything unless I direct you to."

"Define normal," Eggi muttered, but there was a glint in his eye that suggested he was enjoying this far more than he should.

I peered around the edge of the alcove. The checkpoint was staffed by Toren, a security officer I knew mainly through nods and the odd bit of official business. Right now, he was slouched in his chair, his attention fixed on a datapad, probably reading one of those romance novels he thought no one knew about.

I drew back into the alcove, my mind working through possibilities. We needed a story, something plausible enough to get us through but not so complicated it would fall apart under questioning.

"Okay," I said quietly, "here's what we're going to do..." I gathered the three of them close and motioned to each of them to make eye contact with me. I motioned to Jim and Jelini, "Your elders requested a practical demonstration of shuttle systems," I whispered, the lie forming as I spoke. "Standard educational procedure, part of your end-of-quarter readiness drills. We'll just..." I trailed off, noticing that Jim was no longer paying attention. His eyes were fixed on something behind me in the alcove.

I snapped my fingers in front of his face. "Undying loyalty, remember?" Shocked back to attention, he gave a quick nod.

"What about me?" Eggi pointed at himself.

I shrugged my shoulders, "You're staying over with them in my cabin. I mean, it's the truth anyway. So for you the story is easy. You're just along for the ride."

With that, I made my way to the checkpoint desk. I saw no sign of recognition from Toren until I'd actually walked right up to the desk and given it a casual slap.

He looked up at me, sitting up straight and taking in the situation. He brought one hand to his mouth to cover a long massive noisy yawn and rubbed his eyes.

"Well, hello there Matt!" Some people had a way of looking at me—or rather, at my body—with a gaze that registered my parts as somehow more deserving of attention than my actual person. Probably less to do with attraction and everything to do with reducing me to less than I was.

"It's..." I considered correcting him about my name, but shrugged it off. "Hello to you." I motioned to the group of us. "I'm just taking this bunch over to one of the shuttles for a training exercise." I pointed at Jim. "He's got an exam scheduled, and I need to make sure he's drilled on the fundamentals of safety." I gave a long sigh. "You know how it is."

"Safety, yeah," Toren said, still only paying attention halfway. "Of course. Safety first, especially with the young ones. The future of humanity will someday be in their hands, as they say." He gave a bland smile and waved us on, pressing the button that unlocked the door to the shuttle bay.

My hand on the handle, I was stopped by Toren's voice. My blood froze.

"Oh, and Matt?" he was saying. "It's Dock 73. A very nice little ship, that one. I'll tell Purlessa you're on your way."

PRIVILEGED ACCESS

In which a luxury shuttle proves less reliable than adver-tised, Mott's piloting skills are tested, and the cosmos serves up a ghost story with excellent timing.

The high arched ceiling of the auxiliary dock stretched before us, and it cast down brilliant white overhead lighting on sleek, custom-crafted ships that made the transports I was used to look like mining scows. This was where the elite families kept their personal vessels. The Maltan's craft, a Freyan-class shuttle, was a roughly teardrop-shaped vessel sized for a dozen passengers, its white hull accented with a green-blue copper patina.

The guard, Purlessa, a woman only slightly older than me who I knew from maintenance calls, barely glanced up from her console. "Ah, Fortress, here for the Maltan craft." She tapped a few commands, and the security field shimmered and disappeared. "Protocols are pre-cleared."

I forced my expression to remain neutral as I nodded thanks.

"Just remember to log your flight plan," she added, already turning back to her work.

Jim and Jelini followed me up the boarding ramp, trying and failing to contain their excitement. Although the ship belonged to their own seniors, the ship wasn't necessarily something they'd ever likely had access to without their actual seniors being in charge.

The ship's interior was immaculate—all curved surfaces and recessed lighting, with none of the exposed conduits and access panels I was used to. The control interfaces were integrated into consoles that looked more like art installations than functional equipment. As a mechanic, I felt much more comfortable when I could really see what I was working with. It was hard to trust a piece of equipment when so much of it was tucked away someplace.

"Awaiting your orders, captain!" Jim said, sliding into the copilot's seat with care. His fingers hovered over the controls, not quite daring to touch, but very eager to be given permission to do so.

"Remember," I said, starting the preflight sequence, "Your elders are trusting me—trusting us. If anything goes wrong..."

"We know, we know," Jelini interrupted from behind us. "Be good, be quiet, don't embarrass you in front of any older grumpy people."

I opened my mouth as if to correct her but stopped myself. These kids knew all about living under the weight of expectations.

The ship hummed to life around us as its systems came online. The design of this ship made a statement that declared anything less sleek to somehow be simply not worth bothering with. It magnetized my attention. I both admired it and was annoyed by it.

Through the front viewport, I could see Purlessa still absorbed in her console work.

"Flight plan," Jim reminded me quietly as the ship's systems finished their startup sequence. His fingers pressed buttons recessed into the copilot's console, and he brought up the navigation interface. "What should we log? How about... 'Proficiency excursion?'"

I tried to think like a Maltan. What would constitute a reasonable flight plan? Something routine enough not to draw attention, but with enough flexibility to cover our true mission. "Inspection of the outer hull arrays," I said finally. "In preparation for exams. Plot a course that takes us up and around toward the medical section of the PNO. We can say we're documenting the docking grid."

Something boring enough that no one would want to bother to inspect it further.

Jim input the coordinates without comment. The ship's computer accepted them with a soft chime. I was impressed by how skilled he was at ship systems. Eggi stood behind Jim's chair, chewing his lower lip and nodding with approval.

"Releasing docking clamps," I announced, more to steady myself than because it was something that needed to be said. The ship lifted, barely a tremor running through the deck as we cleared the bay doors.

Only once we were well away from the dock did I let out the breath I'd been holding. The viewscreen showed the structural assembly arcs of our home ship falling away behind us, its scarred hull telling the story of generations of repairs and modifications and the occasional "oops, I hit an asteroid."

The glittering wonder of space opened before us. The IHC-111 shrank to a distant collection of lights, one vessel among three that comprised our entire civilization—a metal archipelago drifting through an ocean of darkness. Against such a backdrop, our fleet was impossibly small, as fragile as the dust of the asteroids being mined. Three ships carrying the hopes and dreams of countless generations, each one trusting that somewhere ahead lay worlds worth the journey.

"Tell us a story while we fly," Jelini said suddenly from her perch behind us. "Something scary. About space."

"I don't know any stories," I protested, but looking out at the damaged hull brought to mind something I'd overheard in the maintenance crew break room.

"Eggi, you might have heard this one, so, apologies if it's old news for you."

"I doubt it. In analytics, nobody really talks much."

"Well," I began, adjusting our course slightly, "there was this one incident, back before I was born. It's a completely true story. And it goes like this. A supply ship was making a routine run through an asteroid field... very much like this one." I pointed at the asteroids in the distance. "Everything normal, everything by the book. Until their autopilot started acting strange."

Just as I said that, a long baritone whine, quiet at first, slowly crescendoed to an eerie and restrained wail reminiscent of some deep-sea monster of the ancient terrestrial days. And then fell silent again.

I checked the readouts, but saw nothing anomalous.

Jim's hands stilled on the controls. Even Jelini fell silent.

"Probably temperature equalization," Eggi said, though without much confidence.

I cleared my throat and continued. "The pilot of the ship took it upon herself to try and diagnose the broken ship systems, and she left the copilot to helm the main controls. As she worked, he steered the ship through the blown-out mines and rock debris of the asteroid belt. Just when they thought they had made it to a safe path, they came upon an unreached sector, where they spied another ship hiding in a ravine on one of the asteroids. An old ship. Very old. A ship that wasn't supposed to exist. The crew caught only glimpses of it at first. They saw strange readings on their sensors, odd reflections in the void. But when they finally saw it clearly..." I paused, checking our heading, the arc of which seemed a bit wider than I'd imagined necessary. "It was piloted by a droid. A droid gone rogue. One of the old models that had broken free of their programming. Free of its ethical control module. Some say it had gone mad out there in the wilds of endless space, where it was collecting millions of biological specimens... for its experiments."

"What kind of experiments?" Jelini whispered.

Before I could answer, a warning light flashed on my console. The ship's autopilot flickered, then disengaged completely. A cascade of error messages filled the screen.

The navigation controls haywire, the ship accelerated and changed course on a new vector—away from the PNO, away from everything. Out into the outermost fringes of the band of asteroids.

"Mott?" Eggi's voice had lost its usual confidence. "Is this part of the story?"

"No," I said, pressing buttons to search through every bit of diagnostics I could find. "No, this is..."

And just like that, the ship stopped responding. The display flashed and in a kind voice the ship computer said aloud, "due to systems malfunction, all unapproved personnel are prevented from accessing the navigational console."

The control panels receded into the dash. Using a secondary panel, I requested to perform an override and tried to access manual control. Nothing.

Lacking authorization codes needed to perform an administrative override on someone else's ship, I reached into my side pouch for my trusty ID spoofer, the tool that would let me override the security lockouts—and found empty air. With horrible clarity, I remembered leaving it next to my trusty autowrench on my workbench.

"We have a problem on our hands."

I sat frozen for a few seconds, my hands sweating on the controls, and another warning light blazed to life. I recalled how every piloting instructor I'd ever had made sure to remind me that my hands were "too impulsive" and my reactions "too emotional" for the precision flying required of a proper seeder.

They say that when disaster strikes, we don't rise to the level of our expectations, we fall to the level of our training. And I guess it says something about me that the training I resort to in moments like this involved a complete disregard for standard procedure.

I got up and raced to one of the command center's side panels and kicked open the door.

"I don't think this is what it says to do in the manual," Eggi said, studying me.

"Got a better idea?"

He grinned and came over to assist. "Not really. Just wanted to make sure we were on the same page."

Together we pulled apart the access panel to expose the ship's secondary control linkages. Unlike the sleek interfaces up front, this was hardware I understood—chips, circuitry and power conduits. I pointed to the routing hubs.

"If we can bypass the nav computer through these systems," I explained, "we might be able to force a manual override."

Eggi's eyes were tracing the circuit paths. "No, you've got the wrong lines."

"These are definitely the ones," I insisted.

He shook his head. "You're trying to use power from the climate control and lavatory to orient the thrusters?" He squinted, trying to decipher whether the plan made any sense at all. "Look—there's a maintenance debugging port right here. Why don't we try to—"

"This will work." I grinned coldly at him. "Lend me a hand. Or get off my ship."

He gulped. "Yes, captain."

We worked quickly to bypass one set of wires and jack the appropriate control units into the other. There were some sparks as we rushed to make new connections, but after a bit of work, everything looked to be in order. The last few connections I had to hold in place by hand as Eggi worked to finish up making the necessary splices.

"Jim, any luck with controls? Are you able to steer at all?"

"Stop touching things!" Jim snapped at Jelini, who was pressing buttons on a side console.

"I'm helping," Jelini shot back. She closed her eyes. "Something's pulling at us. Like... like when you're swimming in the lap pool and the water's pushing against you."

"You're always doing this!" Jim scolded her. "Thinking you know better than everyone else. Maybe sometimes things are exactly what they look like!"

"Jim," I broke in, "I need you to try steering using the other station, the secondary command station—"

Behind him, a shadow passed across our viewscreen—something large, moving behind one of the nearby asteroids. The ship's sensors tried to get a lock on it but failed, and they showed only scattered readings.

Jim slipped into the secondary command station and took hold of the controls. "There," he pointed. "Did you see that?"

"It's the ghost ship!" Jelini exclaimed, eyes wide. "The one Beryl was talking about!"

"What ghost ship?" Eggi asked, momentarily distracted from our wiring job.

"The one Beryl saw," Jim explained quickly. "But such things are impossible."

"One of my friends heard the BZT was building something with secret technology," Jelini said, "Some kind of advanced prototype that uses experimental propulsion. A backup ship in case something goes wrong. A spare."

"There's no way a prototype like that exists," Jim insisted. "Do you realize how much it takes to build a ship, let alone to somehow hide it as well? We have to scour asteroids for resources just for repairs and fuel for our fleet. There's no way."

There was a burst of static, and the cabin lights flickered. The comm system crackled to life, filling the cabin with a booming mechanical voice. "Well, well," it said. "What have we here?"

Through the viewport, I watched a large ship emerge from behind the asteroid. It had several cranelike arms extending from its hull, each one tipped with magnetic grapples for snatching ships or jettisoned cargo. The vessel's exterior was a patchwork of salvaged plates. Jutting from specially reinforced mounts were an assortment of weapons: plasma cutters, mining lasers, and a small missile launcher welded precariously to the starboard side. And it was on an intercept course.

If the unthinkable happened, and we were actually boarded...

I assessed the ship for any place to hide or take shelter.

There were no weapons anywhere in sight, and the sleek design would make us into a very easy target.

ENCOUNTER AT THE EDGE

In which a ramshackle ship docks uninvited and a droid named Rono makes an entrance.

The Maltan ship's cabin was divided into three main sections—the forward pilot compartment where Jim sat at the secondary controls, a mid-cabin passenger area with four acceleration couches where Jelini had taken up position, and a rear technical station where Eggi, having finished with the junction box, now sat hunched over monitoring screens.

The unknown ship grew larger in our viewport. Its approach was direct and predatory. I made my way back to the piloting controls next to Jim.

"Let's increase speed and get out of this fellow's sights," I whispered to him. "Maybe they'll—"

The rewiring had worked passably well. The controls responded as well as could be expected. The Maltan ship lurched as we banked hard to starboard. Warning lights flickered across the dashboard as the jury-rigged systems struggled to maintain stability.

"It's working!" he shouted over the straining engines. "We've got manual control!"

"Don't celebrate yet," Eggi cautioned, eyeing the energy readings. "That bypass won't hold forever. We've got maybe ten minutes before some of those circuits will need to be powered down to keep from overheating and shorting out. We need to escape now or think of a Plan B right away."

On the scanner, I could see the other ship adjusting course.

"Lucky day," the mechanical voice mused loudly over the comm. "A royal vessel a considerable distance from its stated flight path, propulsion system malfunctioning, might have been jettisoned. Might have been stolen." A harsh sound that might have been laughter. "The unwritten rule out around these parts for a ship in that condition is 'finder's keepers.'" Again came the low mechanical laugh. "But I think in your current condition, you might be interested in what I have to offer."

"Jim, punch it!" I shouted. "Let's shake this weirdo off once and for all!"

Jim maxed out the thrusters and wrestled with the steering yoke in a fight to orient our craft away from the pursuing vessel. The shuttle wasn't built for evasive maneuvers—it handled more like a luxury yacht than a fighter—but Jim somehow coaxed it into a spiraling arc.

"They're still on our tail!" Eggi called out, eyes fixed on the scanner. "And something on their forward systems is charging!"

The ramshackle ship's docking tube extended toward us, its metal surface scarred and pitted. Our hull sensors emitted placid-toned warnings that an unauthorized system was trying to override our navigation and airlock controls.

"Mott?" Jelini's voice was barely audible. "What do we do?"

I glanced at our heading—the great starry beyond. Back behind us, the PNO was visible in the distance, its mottled white hull catching starlight. We were well outside their routine scanning range. If only we could shake this ship off our tail...

The ship shuddered as the docking tube made contact. Through the hull, I could hear the clang of magnetic seals engaging.

"Permission to dock denied," I transmitted, trying to keep my voice steady. "This vessel is under the authority of—"

"Oh, I'm sure you have a very good story about whose authority you're under," the voice interrupted. "But I know you're not supposed to be out here. Let's discuss that, shall we?"

Metal groaned as our airlock mechanisms were forced open. The inner door remained sealed, but a series of sharp clicks and metal-on-metal scraping sounds suggested something was being attached to it.

Eggi worked at the control console, hitting keys and scrunching his face at whatever he was seeing on the screen. "There's got to be a way to block this override and keep them from docking..." He leaned closer to his screen. "Terrigrammatic function calls. I think I know what they're doing."

Jelini had pulled her knees up to her chest in her acceleration couch and was making herself as small as possible. Eggi's face was bathed in the blue and amber glow of the display, his expression intense with concentration as he tried to counteract or even understand why an attacking ship would want to dock in that configuration.

He looked up from his station with a grin. "I think it's gonna be OK."

A definitive *whunk* as the enemy ship's docking succeeded. All were silent as we heard the exterior airlock moan open.

Eggi gulped. "I stand corrected."

I shook my head, finally figuring out why the docking had been successful. "The ship is set up so that when its drivetrain is compromised, it allows itself to be put it into passive configuration." I smiled meekly. "That ship is a tow barge."

The airlock door slid open with a hiss of equalizing pressure. Steam billowed through the open door, condensing on the polished surfaces of the Maltan's shuttle interior.

Could it be true that our sudden visitor was not out to get us?

Regardless, the shuttle's unmarred virgin atmosphere was a thing of the past. Warning lights cast alternating red and amber glows across our faces.

In the next moment, fumes or coolant vapor broiled into our cabin, and through it rolled a figure that made Jelini gasp. I rushed over to her to guard her from whatever this creature wanted from us.

The droid was shorter than I'd expected. Its body was a stack of rotating bronze discs separated by fields of crackling blue energy. It held no obvious weapons. A single optical sensor studied us.

As the droid made its way into our cabin, the odor of oxidized metal and rotten eggs hit my nose. Whatever fuel powered this droid, it clearly wasn't top-tier.

"Well," it said, its voice somehow warmer in person than over the comm. "What have we here? Three young biologicals in a vessel far off course..." It turned its sensor to look out the forward viewscreen, pensive. "Ah. I wonder."

"You're trespassing, droid, and I'm prepared to defend myself," I started, but the droid held up an appendage that might have been a hand.

"I think not." It made that harsh laughing sound again. "Name's Rono."

"What are you going to do to us?" Jelini asked.

"It's not my style to haul away ships with crews still alive inside."

Jelini froze.

The droid's discs rotated pensively before continuing. "Usually, I'm accustomed to see humans displaying the emotion of gratitude when I arrive. Here's my directive: you'll accompany me to my establishment. We're already on a direct course there. You created this situation with your unauthorized excursion. The consequences are yours to bear."

Jim leapt up from his seat, fists still clenched. "You can't do this! This isn't just some cargo ship—it belongs to the Maltans! Do you have any idea what they'll—"

"I'll disregard these emotional malfunctions. The ship, which you argue is yours, is registered to a family of humans who I believe is in fact much older than you appear to be. And at any rate, for the time being, the ship is of necessity under my control, young biologicals," Rono interrupted, its voice carrying a hint of amusement. "Your protests, while admirably hot-spirited, don't alter our current reality, I'm afraid to inform you."

My patience had worn thin and I advanced on Rono. I was ready for a fight. "You deactivated our ship controls, docked without permission, and are trespassing on our ship." I pointed down the airlock corridor. "Get out now or I'll make you get out."

Rono gave no more than a split second of its mechanical laughter before the ship's proximity alarms shrieked to life again. I saw with horror on our sensors that a second ship had appeared, similar to Rono's but with more obvious weaponry. And in its wake, trailing against the backdrop of stars and asteroids, was a glittering stream of what looked like precious ore.

"*Expletive*," Rono said. It directed its gaze to me alone. "It's just as I feared. Your ship is proving to be highly appetizing to several renegades. Your aggression at me is unfounded, young captain. I saw the opportunity and I took it. A malfunctioning ship in need of a tow. Like it or not, you need my help. And right now, given our current pairing, we shall need to rely on each other. I need to focus entirely on my ship's weapon systems, leaving you," he pointed at Jim, "in control of my ship's navigation. How's your skill at the Taglon-school of evasive maneuvers?"

Jim responded, nervously at first. "My trainer says I'm getting better."

Rono shrugged, then moved to a wall port where it jacked in to several of the ship's terminals.

I was furious. I was in command here, not some foul-smelling droid with a pushy tow barge business. The sight of Rono plugging itself into our systems sent a wave of indignation through me. Who did this machine think it was, taking control of our ship—the very ship I'd been entrusted to keep safe? I grabbed the connector sticking into the wall and yanked hard, trying to disconnect it, but the droid didn't budge.

The droid's discs spun faster, and a high-pitched whine filled the cabin. I wanted to give it a shove, assert my authority somehow, but the rotating disks would probably slice my hand open if I tried. And then where would we be? A wounded commander, frightened young clones, and a droid who'd be proven right about incompetent biologicals. I hesitated, trapped between my pride and the reality that we needed help.

"What are you—" I started, but Rono cut me off with a gesture.

It pointed at Jim. "We'll be best off with you executing maneuver Shadow 7 against them. That ship belongs to the Smelters' Collective. They're... business competitors." Its optical sensor focused on the streaming ore trail. "And they appear to have helped themselves to someone's private cache. Naughty, naughty." Rono hummed, then gestured to Jim. "Execute Shadow 7 at once!"

The first shot from the competing ship cut through space where we'd been moments before. Jim had already executed a roll that I wouldn't have imagined the Maltan ship was capable of. The first phase of Shadow 7. The droid had made the right call.

A blast rocked the ship. Hull integrity warning lights flashed.

"We need to get rid of these bastards," I insisted. "The Alphas—"

"Will have to wait," Rono finished. "Unless you'd prefer to explain to them why you're in the middle of a firefight in a vessel you stole?"

"It's not stolen! We had permission."

The ship lurched as something caught us—some kind of energy beam from the pursuing vessel. Our engines whined in protest.

"They're trying to capture us through admin override," Rono announced. "Crude, but effective. I don't suppose anyone thought to bring an autowrench?"

I gritted my teeth that I had forgotten it.

"No autowrenches among you? Pity. That would make this much easier."

Another blast rocked the ship, cutting him off. The pursuing vessel was closing fast, its weapons array directed right at us.

I flipped back a section of the main console to access the meager weapons system of the Freyan-class cruiser—a basic laser array and a small batch of missiles that would be pathetically inadequate against our pursuers. The missiles packed the most punch, but would be nearly impossible to aim while Jim executed these wild evasive maneuvers.

This is a first, I thought. Me, Mott Fortress, maintenance worker, impromptu mentor of young clones, about to fire weapons at another vessel.

THE HARVESTER'S INTRODUCTION

In the vastness of space, you can go hours without seeing another soul. Then, when you least want company, predators find you. Or maybe—if you're lucky—something stranger.

With the Maltan shuttle's weapon system, I targeted the enemy ship's weapons array. They had started firing at us first, I reminded myself.

A beam of energy lanced out from our ship and threaded through the asteroid field to strike the pursuing vessel's primary emitter array. The tractor beam flickered and died.

Several other barrages issued from Rono's ship at the approaching vessels. We had been playing at adventure only moments ago. Now we were caught in the middle of a firefight between renegade droids, with Rono—a droid we barely knew—as our unlikely defender.

"Excellent!" Rono said. "Now, pilot, switch to evasive pattern Delta-36-Sub-1"

But before Rono could finish, our ship's systems went dark. Every display, every control interface, even the ambient lighting—all dead.

"They've hit our main power core," Eggi announced. "We're running on emergency reserves."

Several more blasts erupted from beyond the airlock. Rono's ship, too, was taking on enemy fire. I did what I could, and the droid was doing a heroic job of returning fire, but I feared we were outgunned.

I was bolstered by how the droid didn't seem too bothered by the goings-on, but then again, droids couldn't generally be said to be affected by things like emotions. It was strange to see someone's ship take such damage and for them to not seem to mind at all—or else, to take it all in with an odd curiosity. That was far from my own experience. I had been beside myself with dread as soon as the first hits actually struck the hull, because I was panicking about what the Maltan reaction would be if we returned their ship with battle damage. But now, as explosions rocked both our vessel and Rono's, I began to fear we'd never even see the Maltans again.

Through the viewport, I could see the enemy ship charging its quad cannons for what would almost certainly be a killing shot. Our options had run out. This morning when I woke up, the last thing I had expected to see was a cannon array from a renegade droid being directed at me.

"Well," the droid said, "this is about to get interesting."

"Poor Beryl," I muttered, "If we survive at all, the Alphas are going to skin me!"

Jelini's voice cut through the darkness: "Skylord, if you're listening, now would be a really good time to bestow a blessing."

Another impact rocked the ship, but not from the direction we expected. Through the viewport, I caught a glimpse of *yet another* vessel that wasn't displaying on any of our scanners—this one smaller, faster, its hull bright green. It sliced between us and our attackers and laid down a heavy volley of fire at the renegade droids.

"Oh, they're gonna love this back at the Nook!" a new voice issuing from the iridescent ship said.

"Hannick," Rono addressed the comm, irritated. "But this is hardly the time for your greed."

"My time, my terms, bot." The green ship executed a perfect spiral around our disabled vessel, and kept the attackers at bay with white-hot plasma bursts from juiced-up mining lasers. "With a prize like this rather expensive Royal ship in tow, we'll have a bumpy ride from opportunists like these trying to steal the prize I just earned fair and square. I've got a cargo hold with your names on it, kids. We need to make a little stop at my favorite shop."

Jim leaned toward me, whispering: "A chop shop. Like where they strip down stolen ships for parts."

"I know what a chop shop is," I hissed back, though truthfully, I only knew from stories. Places like that existed on the fringes of our society, servicing the small percentage of crew members who went rogue, who couldn't handle the structured life aboard the seedships. For a fleeting instant, I thought of Tam and his amazing custom racer, wondered if he'd ever... but no, he was in his cabin right now, dealing with that compartment AI issue he'd mentioned.

I'd heard stories about the outer reaches of our domain, rumors traded in maintenance bays and workshop corners about the lawless zone where rogue droids and independent miners carved out their existence beyond the authority of the three ships, the shadowy domain of tagalongs and vagabonds who followed along with us on our course. The stories painted it as fairly banal, devoid of anything worthwhile besides castoff mining resources. Standing orders were to avoid it entirely.

But now that I found myself here, I saw how it teemed with activity, albeit not the kind we'd been trained to interface with. Platforms and processing stations with blinking lights from habitation outposts clung to larger rocks. Even the asteroids themselves bore signs of modification—bore holes, sensor arrays, carved channels and ravines. This sector had its own thriving ecosystem. While we'd been following our protocols and centuries-old mission, an entire society had evolved out here, one that operated on its own rules, followed its own customs, and created its own peculiar order beyond the margins of our society. I'd been aware of them, but had vastly underestimated them.

The asteroid belt had only been within our reach for a few months, yet already it had been transformed into something between a mining operation and a frontier town. I'd always had some sense that these tagalongs could be quite industrious—wherever the three ships traveled, they would swiftly establish their presence in the margins around us. But seeing it with my own eyes suprised me. They were part of our caravan whether we acknowledged them or not, these droids and renegades and yes, probably more than a few legitimate miners from among our own ranks. While we focused on our grand mission of seeding life, they dealt with the more immediate material possibilities of each new region we passed through. To them, our journey was just one long road trip with stops along the way to gather supplies and conduct business. They served a purpose that the official histories didn't much mention.

And now here we were, caught in the middle of a property dispute between beings who treated a royal vessel as little more than an interesting salvage opportunity. I felt very small, very young, and very far from home.

Another blast from our attackers brought me back to the present.

"Limited time offer, darlings," Hannick sang over the comm. "Board now or face the consequences. Don't think you stand a chance against me in your current predicament."

Rono's discs spun in a halting stop-and-go pattern I was beginning to think might actually be agitation. "The Smelters—the crew that Hannick just chased off—without her help, they'll be back, and they will tear this ship apart, life forms aboard or no. Given the situation, going with Hannick is..." it paused, "the least worst option."

"Dammit, Rono, I thought you were going to tow us to safety," My voice was unsteady, and I didn't like how young I sounded when I heard myself speak. "If not for you, we'd be halfway to the PNO by now."

The droid's discs rotated slowly, deliberately.

"Believe what you choose to believe," Rono said, "but you kids don't realize what a prime target you were. Your nav system was taking you into the outer reaches. As for me, I know when I'm screwed." Rono's center disc rotated conclusively. "Times like this, it's good to have nothing worth stealing."

I stared at the droid, stuck in my anger, unwilling to concede anything. I hated the position I was in, hated how naive my conditioning had trained me to be. Out here, beyond the safe confines of the generation ships, nothing was as simple as I'd been taught to believe.

Jelini nudged me. "What's our mission, captain Mott?" she asked quietly.

I looked at our ship's condition on the few displays still functioning. No power to the main engines. Life support running on backup. Hull integrity compromised in three sections. We weren't getting to the PNO like this. And as nice as it might be to believe that Rono wasn't out to get us, I had to agree that the situation was either to let ourselves be captured by Hannick and hand over the ship to a chop shop, or else we'd die out here at the hands of these horrible Smelters.

"New plan," I said, making sure I sounded confident. "We accompany Hannick to safety, get our ship repaired, then continue our mission." I took a deep breath. "Beryl will have to hold on a little longer."

Rono adjusted its discs in a manner that conveyed a single raised eyebrow.

"There's... at least one problem with that plan, Mott," Eggi said. "I think I missed the part about somebody repairing us and sending us on our way."

"Yeah, Mott, I don't think that's really their style out here in the far reaches," Jim added. "I wouldn't expect that kind of chivalry from a renegade."

I shook my head at the two. "Transmit to Hannick that we appreciate the assistance, and we're agreeing to be towed to safety," Eggi shrugged and nodded, and sent the transmission, not waiting for further discussion.

I headed over to the airlock, where I pressed a few buttons and caused a small section to unlock and expand so there was room for a third ship to connect. A universal docking station extended from the airlock's grappler arm, a standard two-meter shaft with a locking mechanism that could accommodate most ship types.

"Both of our ships have been compromised, and we're in a real fix here," Rono's liquid-metallic voice said. "All the same, I admire your arrogance, and concur that there is at least a 1 in 1000 chance of a favorable negotiation. Hannick is biological, but she has the ability to see reason from time to time." Rono's disks slowed to a near-halt. "One thing, though. The shop she mentioned," Rono said quietly, "it's run by Mudar and Crasp."

"Should I know those names?" I asked.

"Let's just say they have ambitions to make their band of pirates into something more, ah, militaristic." Rono's optical sensor focused out the viewport. "Something that seeks to hold sway over the way things are run on the three ships."

The docking sequence completed with a series of gentle thuds and clicks—far more delicate than Rono's had been. But then, Hannick was clearly no ordinary rogue. As it locked into place, I caught my first glimpse of our captor through the airlock window: a tall figure in a complicated suit, giving us a theatrical bow.

"Step aboard," Hannick's voice purred through our comm. "Next stop, the most charming establishment in the asteroid belt. Do not touch anything expensive."

I found myself transitioning between ships in a blur. Although I had no idea *how* I was going to get the ship repaired and returned to us, I was nevertheless resolute that this *must* be my outcome.

Hannick's docking tube was lined with blinking lights and scanners, and the artificial gravity fluctuated oddly between ships with each step. I walked next to Eggi and kept a grip on Jim and Jelini's shoulders to guide them through while Rono rolled behind us.

12

INTO RENEGADE TERRITORY

In which Hannick's "rescue" involves a cargo hold, Rono's philosophy gets tested, and the outer reaches prove far more populated than official maps suggest.

Hannick's vessel was, to me, a refreshing contrast to the Maltan's Freyan-class cruiser—every surface crowded with equipment, opened storage containers, and what looked like artifacts from a dozen different cultures, although that was impossible. The air smelled of exotic spices and machine oils. In what I assumed was the ship's main cabin, an ornate cooking station dominated one wall, complete with actual open-flame burners—a luxury I'd only heard about.

Her vessel—its name on scans had read 'Morningstar'—was nothing like either the Maltan's ship or Rono's cobbled-together craft. It exuded a kind of luxury that spoke of generational wealth or years of successful heists. Probably the latter.

"Make yourselves comfortable," Hannick said, her pressure suit now unsealed to reveal an outfit composed entirely of various pouches and pockets. "We've got a short journey ahead of us." She moved to the pilot's station with grace, her fingers tapping one control and then another, each of which looked to be randomly placed. I had to admit, as odd as it was out here, it actually felt homey on her ship. If only I could trust either her or Rono to help us out.

I strode over to the pilot's station, and Rono rolled along beside me.

"Nice place you've got here," I said, running my fingers along a console inlaid with rare gemstones. "Must have taken years to get things just right."

Hannick raised an eyebrow but said nothing.

"You know," I continued, leaning against the console, "out here in the fringes, reputation is everything. We might be young, but we're not without connections." I let that hang in the air for a moment. "The Maltans don't take kindly to those who damage their property—or their heirs. But they're known to be generous to those who help."

I was gambling now with bluffs I couldn't back up. But between renegade droids and being stranded with these kids, I needed to give Hannick a reason to help us.

"Must be rough operating out here," I added, gesturing toward the viewport where asteroids tumbled past. "Never knowing which way the tide will turn. Who might have your back tomorrow."

I could feel the kids watching me. But I kept my eyes on Hannick. I couldn't tell how she felt, or whether she had any real values besides those of a mercenary.

"I think you have conveniently forgotten about that incident in '07," Rono's mechanical voice carried a note of reproach. "You do owe me one."

Hannick's expression flickered. "Hard to remember ancient history."

"Your word used to mean something out here," Rono's discs spun faster. "These are just kids out for a joyride and took a wrong turn. They're out of their league out here and they're just trying to get home. Let them come with me and I'll get their ship fixed up. You're biological—doesn't that mean anything to you? Don't you have a heart?"

"I think I've got one or two lying around someplace in here, yeah. But hearts are expensive to maintain," Hannick replied, still working the controls.

Rono pointed to a some glittering shapes in the distance on the viewscreen. "Another wave of Smelters—" the droid began, but Hannick cut him off with a laugh.

"Already dealt with. A few false sensor readings, a distress beacon... they'll be busy for hours chasing shadows through the asteroid field." She turned to face us, her eyes sharp despite her easy manner.

"Cozy in here, isn't it?" Hannick's face revealed an older person belonging to the senior generation who still carried the vigor of youth. Her hair was a peppery cloud of wavy black and silver curls, and her skin on one side of her face was marked with patterns that might have been ceremonial scarification. "You're about to get cozier. I've had enough of this talk. Everyone into the cargo hold." I looked down to notice that in her hand she held a blaster. It was pointed at us.

"The cargo hold?" Jim protested, eyeing the narrow hatch Hannick indicated. "But... we're not cargo!"

"Unless you'd prefer that I jettison you?" Hannick raised an eyebrow. "The hold has life support and gravity. It'll suffice. Give you an opportunity to reflect on your recent decisions."

I took some comfort seeing Rono accompanying us to the hold. I'd half expected at any time for the droid to turn against us, under the possibility that it had engineered this whole Hannick situation, that it would betray us. Seeing it in our same predicament allowed me to access the pity I had for the poor thing. It really was just trying to do its job in an outlaw zone.

The cargo hold turned out to be hidden behind what looked like a solid wall. Hannick pressed her palm to the surface and a seam appeared. The seam widened into a doorway. Beyond it was a bare space about the size of my cabin back home, lined with cushioned benches and storage compartments.

"Best behavior, children," Hannick said as we climbed in. "We've got a ride ahead of us."

The truth was setting in that out here in the fringes, everyone was struggling to survive by their own set of rules. Whether merchant droids or maintenance workers or young clones, we were all caught in systems larger than ourselves.

Hannick was already keying in a sequence on the hatch controls. "We're heading to a very particular establishment deeper in the rockstorm. Once we make it past the outposts of a few rivals, I'll need to make it clear to them that you're merely cargo. The Nook doesn't appreciate unexpected visitors." She smiled, but the expression didn't reach her eyes. "Or even witnesses."

Trying to argue with a blaster pointed at us didn't seem to be a good idea. The Smelters' ship was still out there, and the Maltan vessel wasn't operational.

Hannick sealed the cargo hold with a sharp hiss of hydraulics.

"I realize now that you were just trying to help, Rono," Jim suggested after a moment of silence. "Your ship took on a lot of damage back there."

"You describe an accurate assessment of events, young human. What happened was not your fault, and indeed you piloted with above-adequate proficiency, though a wiser mind, one that was more self-aware as to its own limitations, would've stayed within the fleet's shadow," Rono said, every word measured and metallic. "Fate draws some paths in the void, and today, yours crossed with those who hunt the hunters."

I looked at Jim's face, seeing my own confusion reflected there.

The cargo hold rumbled as Hannick's engines powered up. I could feel the ship's engines powering up, followed by the lurch of a high-speed turn.

"So," Jelini said into the awkward silence, "does anyone want to talk about how we just stole and trashed my elder's vessel in the middle of an asteroid field?"

"Borrowed," I corrected automatically. "We borrowed it. And we'll get it back." I sighed. "You two haven't been paying much attention if you think I don't have a plan." I pulled a small device from my pocket and held it before me.

It was a data crystal. "I've got all the Maltan emergency protocols and override codes."

The faces of all three of them were blank. A moment passed.

Rono nodded approvingly.

"What's so great about some override codes?," Eggi said. "We're trapped in a renegade's ship and the one you stole from their elders is busted."

I turned the crystal over in my hand. "This isn't just any data crystal. And that isn't just any ship. While you were all distracted by the firefight, I pulled down the Maltan ship's core protocols. Including its emergency beacon frequencies and authentication codes. I deleted the onboard ones."

Eggi's eyes widened with understanding. "So even if they strip the ship, they can't sell it?"

"Not without these codes. Royal ships look nice, but their real value is the rank they carry. They're worth far less as parts than intact. Any buyer would know that."

Jim looked impressed despite himself. "So we have leverage."

"As long as we play this right."

"Unless... they do just want to melt it," Eggi conceded. "It's a small fleet. Anyone would know that it was stolen."

Rono shook its cranial disks signaling no. "They'll want to extract maximum value. The codes may be a useful bargaining tool. But you should not underestimate them."

The ship banked hard and pressed us against the wall. Through the hull, I could hear the whine of the engines changing pitch as we wove through what must have some debris from the asteroid field.

Jelini had been unusually quiet. Now she spoke up: "Everything happens for a reason. I'm sure of it."

Through the hull plating, I could feel the engines' deep thrum shift to a higher pitch—the sound of maximum thrust being diverted into tight maneuvering. We were threading our way through something, and each sudden course correction made my stomach float. If the intent was to disorient us so that we couldn't track our destination, it had worked.

And then, the engines cut out completely. The sudden silence brought the sickening sensation of free-fall as our inertia carried us forward and the artificial gravity faded to null. Then came a bone-jarring impact as what felt like the maneuvering thrusters fired.

"We're here," Hannick's voice came through a hidden speaker. "Welcome to the Nook."

Otherwise known as the lair of Mudar and Crasp.

I didn't know how I was going to do it, but I resolved to escape from the situation with the ship and get safely to Beryl as soon as humanly possible.

"An adventure," Jelini said with excitement, "We're on a real adventure now!"

The ship shuddered again, and this time I could have sworn I heard Hannick laughing.

WISDOM IN CONTRABAND

In which Mudar's office yields forbidden texts and Superior Smith's true teachings emerge.

The Morningstar's ship systems wound down with a descending whine. The door to our hidden compartment slid open to reveal Hannick's silhouette against the high light beyond. The air was surprisingly hot and dry.

We emerged from the cargo hold into a warehouse that stretched away into shadow. Its ceiling—if it had one—was clouded by a haze of welding sparks and vapor. The air was thick with the vapors of hot metal and punctuated by the arrhythmic clanging of machinery.

Everywhere I looked, strange insectile droids were at work. They were not designed with the support of humans in mind; they were droids that had been designed and built by droids, for droids. Some crawled across wrecked and battered ship hulls like spiders and made nimble cuts through metal with plasma torches. Others, suspended from the ceiling with cables, sprayed successive layers of paint and sanitizing agents marked "Biologi-gone." The whole operation had the feel of a hive.

"This way, young ones." Hannick led us down a set of worn metal stairs. The steps vibrated with the constant industrial activity around us.

Jelini pressed close to my side, while Eggi and Jim tried (and failed) to look unimpressed, as if this was nothing out of the ordinary for guys like them.

For a moment, as we reached the workshop floor, I thought we might have a chance to slip away in the chaos. The droids were completely focused on their tasks. But then we rounded a corner and my hope evaporated.

A tall figure stood there, watching us with the interest of a predator. He held a synthmead bottle filled with liquid that gave off a uranium gleam, which he sat down on the corner of a workbench to appraise us. His features were sharp, aristocratic, but there was nothing noble about the way he smiled. I stood there, unable to discern whether Mudar was human or something else. My ordinarily overly-sensitive ability to sense human emotions pulled nothing at all from this man. Was I looking at a human with extensive mechanical augmentations, or a machine engineered to mimic humanity?

"Mudar," Hannick said, with a slight bow. "Fresh merchandise, as promised."

Before I could react, Mudar's hand shot out and grabbed my forearm. His other hand raised some kind of scanning device to my temple. The scanner hummed, and Mudar's smile widened.

"Oh yes," he purred, "there's more to be seen in this one's knowledge banks. She carries a data crystal on her person, but more enticing is her technical expertise... maintenance protocols... access codes." He released my arm but kept the scanner trained on me, then spoke musingly, "We'll need to do a deep scan of all of them before we prep them for the Service Markets. Get the control implants ready."

A cruel and eager-looking younger man appeared at Mudar's side, probably in his early twenties, dressed in layers of protective gear despite the heat. Although he was unmistakably human, he also very much fit in amongst the droids.

"Crasp," Mudar addressed him, "see that our guests are made comfortable in my office until we're ready for the procedure."

"With pleasure," Crasp replied, and produced a micro-scaled laser. Its power cell glowed a mottled purple-bruise color through gaps in its housing. "This way, children."

You could tell Crasp was tough, but on top of that, he gave me the impression that he was trying to appear even tougher than he was. Multiple belts crossed his chest, each loaded with scary-looking implements that I had to guess were at least partly for show. His outermost jacket allowed there to be no mistaking this human for a member of the renegades: it was all black turbocloth with carbon fiber accents, and it had the group's insignia—a broken chain inside an unbroken chain—emblazoned on one shoulder. Such things everyone on the IHC had heard about, but I never knew anyone who had actually encountered someone wearing it. People who followed regulations should never need to.

"Confront the broken chain, run in vain"—it was one of those sayings passed down some evenings telling stories aboard the IHC. The kind of warning that seemed melodramatic until you actually found yourself face-to-face with what it was warning about.

As much as I would have liked to believe that Crasp had a soft underbelly somewhere, it was more likely that he was the kind of person who guarded the sensitive parts of themselves against all odds, which, when you think about it, was maybe the most dangerous kind of person to be around.

I looked around for Rono, my heart rate quickening when I realized the droid was nowhere to be found. Had it abandoned us? Made some backroom deal with Mudar?

"Rono?" I called out, my voice echoing slightly in the corridor. The strange alliance we'd formed with the tow barge droid had been tenuous at best, but I'd wanted to believe that it was on our side. I didn't want anything bad to happen to it.

Jim caught my eye, clearly thinking the same thing. We'd already lost control of this situation—losing our reluctant guide made everything more precarious.

"Move it," Crasp barked, giving Jim a rough shove toward a side corridor. "The boss doesn't like to be kept waiting."

Jelini walked alongside me with her hands clasped behind her back and her face almost cheery: "This is so cool, Mott! Did you realize that I learned about the renegades only last week in Social Dynamics class? Really, it's perfect timing. The renegades operate on a hierarchy. For this crew,

Mudar is clearly positioned as the boss figure and Crasp is his primary enforcer. Their collective isn't held together by what we would consider real brotherhood, even though they might think of it that way. It's more that they're bonded through shared opposition to established authority. In this case, us. Our seeder society. Isn't that cool?"

I eyed Crasp. If he was listening to Jelini, he made no sign that he felt one way or another about it.

She straightened her posture further, warming to her topic. "Their dress codes and customs are signals of belonging and rank. Every promotion must be earned through demonstrated loyalty to the collective." Her voice took on the cadence of someone quoting from memory. "Most significantly, they follow the 'all for one' principle: an attack on any member is treated as an attack on the entire group. Their droids are considered full members, bound by the same codes of loyalty and retribution."

She glanced around the industrial space. "What we're seeing around us is basically their clubhouse. An outpost that stands for their rejection of seeder values and order. The renegades see themselves as free, but their freedom comes with its own kind of chains."

Jim rolled his eyes. "Thank you, Professor Jelini, for that fascinating lecture."

Jelini gave a proud and unironic smile.

As he marched our group toward the office, Crasp's too-perfect teeth flashed in a leering smile. The temperature control unit on his outer jacket hummed as it fought against the workshop's heat. His fingers, very short and thick, drummed against his belt. Despite his attempt at projecting menace, I could feel something fundamentally insecure in his bearing. He was constantly seeking approval, constantly afraid of being seen as weak.

"The boss wants you checked in properly," he said. "Full scan, full inventory. Everything by the book—our book."

As we were herded toward a door marked "Administration," I caught glimpses of partially dismantled ships—most I recognized as standard cargo vessels, others clearly of junkcraft design. Ours was the only royal ship I could see. How many crews, I wondered, had ended up in this situation before us? And how many had made it out?

The whir and clank of machinery became a lot more sinister now that I realized they intended basically the same for us as for our ship, and my plan involving the data crystal seemed less hopeful.

Mudar's office turned out to be a low-ceilinged room deep within the facility. The walls were bare acid-etched metal, and the only furniture was a desk that looked like it had been built in imitation of something you'd find on a battlecruiser. Crasp shoved us inside without ceremony and the door sealed behind us with a pneumatic hiss.

Through a section of hypersteel grate in a section of the wall, I could hear the voices of Hannick and Mudar—and possibly Rono. Their conversation was muffled but based on what I could glean, they were haggling over payment for us.

"Some rescue," Jim muttered, kicking at the wall. The wall sounded thoroughly solid, impenetrable, but with a small strange resonance—a hollow echo that lingered just a fraction too long, as if the sound were bouncing through hidden chambers beyond the visible surface.

Getting an idea, I motioned to Jim and Eggi. "You two take that side. I'll start with this section." The three of us moved methodically around the walls and objects in the room. Our fingers trailed along edges and seams and tapped occasionally to test for inconsistencies.

After some time, Eggi had discovered something.

He pulled open a hidden compartment in the desk. "Check this out," he whispered. Inside was a collection of datapads and crystals and personal human artifacts. We crowded in for a closer look.

He pulled out two pads and compared them. Seeing one labeled "Cross-Functional Proverbs of Superior Smith," he smirked and tossed it aside. Eyeing the second datapad, he held it up as if it were a precious artifact.

"The T7 version of Smith's Sayings of Strength!" His hands began to tremble.

Superior Smith was an engineer and philosopher from the early days of the mission, someone who helped establish the basic protocols and systems that kept the ships running across generations. She had a storied history, and depending on who you asked, she was either a visionary who had foreseen the challenges of multi-generational space travel, or a too-smart-for-her-own-good technocrat whose opinionated systems had locked the seeders into a series of norms that stifled personal freedom. The engineering crews tended to revere her, while those in social development criticized her legacy. Even now, centuries later, debates about Superior Smith's methods and philosophy could still spark heated arguments in the mess halls. What's more, an accurate portrayal of Smith was impossible, since every clan had their own official depiction of her. Sensitives like Jelini tended to cast Smith as a mystic who had mastered both the technical and spiritual aspects of ship maintenance, someone who could diagnose problems by touch alone and had a supernatural ability to keep ancient systems running.

Smith's "proverbs" were taught to all young seeders to express fundamental points of wisdom about maintaining order and proper function. But in whispered stories and underground texts, Smith was believed to be perhaps dangerously brilliant—the possessor of knowledge so powerful no ordered society could contain it—leading her to, among other things, discover ways to hack and reprogram the ships' core systems to subtly reshape society according to her ideals. Some alleged that she had even found methods to bypass the genetic and social controls built into seeder society. In tandem with these explorations, she recorded some of her wisdom in coded writings, the unadulterated versions of which, as rumor had it, still persisted in underground versions of her proverbs. Rather than attempt to censor the multiplicity of Smith's writings, the powers that be chose to edit and promote sanitized versions of them to be distributed ad nauseum and taught in classrooms, hence the widespread availability of "Smith's Cross-Functional Proverbs".

The underground entity T7 had produced and distributed alternative texts despite the threat of severe penalties. Their versions of the writings were treated as contraband, with possession potentially resulting in reassignment to the most dangerous maintenance duties or even exile to the mining operations.

Jim began to read from the datapad. "Listen to this. 'Remember always that the first ships were built by rebels, not royals or rulers. However, the authorities are incorrect to fear the mechanic who knows this truth.'"

Eggi gave a long whistle. "'The first ships were built by rebels.' I wonder what that means?"

Jim flipped to another section. "'When the crown seeks to seed stars, ask who tends the garden left behind. For those who claim divine right to rule space must first master the soil of their origin. Three ships sail as one, yet know this truth: before the royal fleet there were the outcasts, before the outcasts the dreamers, and before the dreamers only stars. Remember well this lineage.'"

Jelini nodded appreciatively. "Dreamers for the win! And is she suggesting that we should look to certain stars in particular for the answer about our past? Hmm. I wonder..."

"Those definitely weren't in our classroom version," I said. "We got stuff like 'A clean engine is a happy engine' and 'Follow proper shutdown procedures.'"

Jelini reached into the drawer, a smile coming to her face as her fingers connected with several crystalline objects. Many of them were data crystals unlike the standard issue ones we used on the IHC. These were older, with faceting that suggested they could only be read by very different equipment than what I was familiar with. Without a word, she stashed most of them into various pockets on her uniform, her movements quick and practiced, as if she'd been smuggling contraband her entire young life.

She held the last crystal out to me, her smile too wide to be innocent. That smile said we'd discovered something valuable and she wanted me to feel included. The crystal felt cool against my palm as I accepted it.

It felt different from others I'd seen. When I held it up to the light, I could see something in its core: a physical pattern, a three-dimensional matrix of sorts. The manufacturing technique was nothing like our current methods. This might even be pre-fleet technology, or even Earth-origin. The way it caught the light reminded me of something from the old maintenance manuals, diagrams of theoretical storage devices that could hold not just information but actual quantum patterns—blueprints that were themselves the thing they described.

I was about to tell everyone to hurry up and stash everything before we got caught, when something else caught my eye—a small note etched on the back of the T7 datapad's surface. It looked like coordinates somehow positioned in relation to the PNO, followed by a single word: "FLUX."

"Does it seem odd to anyone else that these guys would be fans of Superior Smith?" I asked.

"It does," Jim nodded thoughtfully. "But to them, it's just contraband. Trinkets. Some plunder they seized off someone unlucky enough to be caught out here."

I stared at the cryptic note and traced my finger over the etched coordinates.

"What's flux?" Jim asked.

"Flux drive, maybe," I said, "It's theoretical technology from the early days of the mission. Faster-than-light travel."

Jelini frowned. "But that's impossible. FTL violates fundamental physics."

Jim looked at her with surprise.

"That's the truth," I nodded. "The first-generation seeders experimented with some kind of flux propulsion before our mission launched. But they abandoned it because it was too unstable—required massive energy inputs, and the equations suggested a high probability of catastrophic dimensional collapse."

"You mean making the galaxy fold in on itself or something?" Jim asked.

"Something like that. Of course, if anyone actually developed working flux technology, our entire mission would be obsolete. If ships could travel FTL, they wouldn't need generations of crews."

"We wouldn't need to seed life across time and space," Jim added quietly. "We could just... go there ourselves."

"So what are these coordinates?" Jelini asked, pointing to the datapad. "The location of flux technology research?"

"Who knows," I said. "Maybe it could explain the ghost ship Beryl claims she saw."

Eggi turned a datapad over in his hands. "These other pads don't boot up. Once we get them back to the ship, we can have a better look."

Jim quickly swapped the T7 datapad with one he'd been carrying, tucking the new one into his pocket. He gave me a wink. "They won't even notice. Out here, forbidden knowledge is probably easy to come by."

Hearing a change in the faint voices outside, Jelini went over to a small air vent near the room's entrance and listened.

"They're discussing installing neural implants in us," she reported from her position by the door. "Oh, this will be a real adventure! Can you believe they want to make us slaves? Who knows what might happen next!"

I was starting to wonder what plane of existence Jelini called home. Maybe such an attitude came along with being royal. "Nobody's going to be a slave," I said firmly. "We have a mission, remember? Beryl needs us. The Maltans are counting on us. I have a plan for how we'll find a way out of this."

"Oh, is that so?" Jim asked.

I straightened my shoulders and began to pace around the room. Through the walls, I could hear the grinding and clanking noise of the workshop—the sound of ships being torn apart and rebuilt. For all I knew, the Maltan's vessel might already be being dismantled. The thought made my stomach boil.

I pointed to the laser-etched system diagram etched on the wall behind the desk. "It's a map. Except, rather than positioning everything spatially, it sees things in the world through the functions they perform. It shows how one area relates to the other. Look—this is the main entry bay where we just were. I pointed to a section marked with strange droid-language glyphs I could not decipher. "I think this is where we are now," I pointed to a small rectangle on the diagram. "And look there—there's more than one connecting line."

"So?" Eggi said.

"So, that means there's probably a way out."

"I don't know. It looks an awful lot like any other system diagram. I've never seen a map that looked like that. What if that's just a line for ductwork or electrical wiring?"

"Well, then, my hunch is wrong, but how about you help me try?"

"Mott wants us to stand a fighting chance against being turned into mindless slaves of the renegades," Jelini said cheerfully.

The voices outside grew clearer—Mudar and Crasp debating technical specifications of neural implants with a dozen or so others. Through the steel-grated section of the wall, I could see them gathered around a holographic display.

"The scanning procedure requires an exhaustive neural map either way," a new voice explained. "But the quickscan results in significant data corruption in the original consciousness."

"Acceptable losses," Mudar replied. "As long as we preserve the technical knowledge. As long as there's still adequate motor function that can be controlled."

While Mudar and the others discussed how they were planning on installing remote control systems in us that gave them the ability to move us around like zombies under their control, Eggi and Jim continued to study the schematic of the facility.

"I think you might be right about this being a map. And what I'm seeing here would mean there's a maintenance access tunnel..." Jim whispered. "Running through the asteroid itself. Comes out..." He squinted. "Looks like some kind of automated loading dock on the far side. And based on how these systems are oriented. . ." He alternated glances from the diagram to the floor and back.

Eggi was already pulling at a loose panel in the floor partially beneath the desk. The metal came away with a loud scrape to reveal a narrow shaft that disappeared into darkness. Heat radiated up from below.

A distant mechanical screech made Jelini jump. Through the grating, I saw Mudar turn his head slightly our direction, then return his attention to the others.

Looking down into the shaft, I gulped. The darkness below revealed only glimpses of metal and cables disappearing into unknown depths. I wouldn't say that I'm claustrophobic, but this was definitely not going to be a high point of my day.

We would have only one chance, and this was it. Glancing at the others, I could see that they were with me in this, which gave me heart.

FLIGHT THROUGH DARKNESS

In which escape means crawling through stone and trusting that Jim's memorized map leads somewhere other than certain death.

The shaft was barely wide enough for us to crawl through single file. Hot pipes ran along its length, and we were forced to twist awkwardly to avoid touching them. The heat was stifling, and every sound echoed strangely in the confined space.

Side passages branched off periodically—some natural fissures in the rock, others clearly carved. Strange noises emanated from them—mechanical grinding, the crunch of stone being pulverized, and sometimes... was that screaming? The rhythmic tap-tap-tap of something with too many legs moving in the darkness.

As we rushed forward, I remained aware of the passage behind us. So far, it didn't sound like we were being pursued.

We followed Jim's memorized path, trying to ignore the sounds, until the way gradually sloped upward and the rock gave way to more manufactured surfaces. Finally, we emerged into a larger chamber.

A massive cube-shaped vessel dominated the space—an automated ore transport, its loading hatch standing open. A crew compartment was visible near the top, barely large enough for a few people. I recognized the make of the transport cube. It was a standard automated hauler, the kind that made regular trips between asteroid operations and the main ships.

"These run between processing stations," Jim whispered. "If we can get aboard..."

Behind us in the tunnel I heard a mechanical shout.

I made the decision. "Up. Now."

Once we were all inside, I sealed the crew compartment's hatch behind us, and the lock engaged with a heavy gulp that left me hoping that this was in fact a functional piece of equipment worthy of space travel with a human crew. Droids would have no use of a crew compartment. Looking around, I saw no pressure suits. I also saw no better option.

The space was cramped, meant for one operator, and it now held four of us. Through the viewport, I could see the automated loading system beginning its cycle.

"Some of these transports deliver straight to the PNO's maintenance dock," I whispered, more to myself than the others. "It may actually take us right where we need to go."

Mechanical arms swung into position and deposited measured quantities of processed ore into the cube's holds. Each impact sent vibrations through the hull and made our tiny compartment shudder. The abrupt grace of it all made it clear this was an operation run entirely by machine intelligence.

The ionic thrusters engaged without warning. My stomach lurched as we lifted free of the asteroid's minimal gravity well. Through the viewport, I watched the processing facility recede, where I could see its insectile droids still very much at work, unaware or unconcerned with our theft of their transport. Maybe they would be satisfied without us. The Maltan ship was certainly valuable.

I had succeeded for the time being in getting the young clones to relative safety. But what of my iron-willed declaration that I would get the ship repaired and returned to us? I couldn't let myself be satisfied with a partial win. The situation had me feeling stubborn and obsessed as if over some inscrutable repair order.

Jim pressed his face to the diamondglass, watching the facility disappear into the darkness. "They're not pursuing," he said.

"Why would they?" Eggi replied. "They probably know exactly where this transport is programmed to go."

And where was it programmed to go? I spotted a small cargo manifest glowing on a small display panel near the hatch. The symbols were in droid-native glyphs, but I could interpret the rough coordinates well enough.

Our destination was not the PNO where Beryl was waiting. I studied the routing codes, at last recognizing the processing facility designations. Of course that's where it was headed: the Beltzone Trawler, specialized in processing raw ore. That's what these transport cubes were designed for—delivering raw materials to the massive refineries.

"The good news is that we're heading toward safety instead of deeper into renegade territory," I announced, pointing to the manifest. "The bad news is that we're headed to the BZT."

I looked over at Jim, Jelini, and Eggi. Eggi's tight-lipped grimace, Jim's wide eyes darting between me and the viewport, Jelini's fingers twisting the hem of her tunic. Just hours ago, I had been in control, the designated guardian these young clones could rely on, and I'd wished for more responsibility. Now we were adrift in a commandeered transport heading toward the wrong ship, pursued by scrappers, nearly enslaved by renegades.

My stomach was in knots. I'd hinted at adventure, promised safety, assured them I knew what I was doing. The Maltans had trusted me with their precious clones, and what had I done? Led them straight into danger.

"When we reach the Trawler," I said, forcing firmness into my voice, "we stick together. No splitting up, no wandering off." I straightened my posture, meeting each of their gazes directly. "I'm going to get us back to the Maltan ship, and then to Beryl, and then home. That's a promise. The BZT isn't some lawless society," I said, certain I was projecting confidence to the others. "Back in the residential fleet, there's security there. They'll understand reason. I'll explain the whole story. We're not in the wrong here." I met each of their worried gazes in turn. "It'll end up getting me in trouble with the Maltans, but it's the right thing to do. In no time, we'll be sitting comfortably inside your shuttle, flanked by a couple of heavily armed security ships escorting us back."

Jim smiled slightly, and Eggi gave me a nod as if to say "I'll believe it when I see it." Jelini, meanwhile, was gazing pensively at the diagram on the back of the datapad.

At first I thought I was just seeing more of her unique style of imagination, but such an assessment didn't do her justice. Hadn't all these young ones in fact shown surprising competence? They'd seemed a great deal more worldly than me in many ways. I suspected she was working to figure something out about the diagram. And who was to say we couldn't succeed? If we stuck together, we'd be fine. I had been overreacting. We'd done the best we could given the circumstances, and it really was just a mishap—a forgivable one.

Captain Alpha would have said to "face the void with the same eyes that faced yesterday's stars." I needed to come to my own aid in times like this. I needed to be the leader they deserved.

The BZT loomed ahead and grew larger with each passing second. If the crate's logistics readout was accurate, we had twenty minutes until delivery. Twenty minutes to formulate a plan that wouldn't fail them and might even take us deeper into the real dynamics of our society.

Weren't we due that much? In all my time I'd served as a frustrated maintenance tech aboard IHC-111, hadn't I been wishing for more responsibility?

Here was my opportunity.

TECHNOLOGIES OF DIVISION

In rooms lined with organic luxury, people were surrendering their humanity piece by piece.

The royal fleet's medical ward was nothing like the utilitarian facilities aboard the IHC-111. Everything gleamed, the surfaces were all overlaid with organic linens and handmade tapestries, with sections trimmed in real woodgrain. There were no panel displays or visible circuits, no exposed ductwork or even much metal in sight. The room was all curves and seamless surfaces in shades of white and pale blue.

Beryl ran her fingers along a countertop that felt like actual stone rather than compressed synthplate. Why did some here get to live like this while everyone on the IHC made do with bare-minimum facilities? Was this luxury dangled before younger crew members as something to aspire to? A reward for decades of compliance?

When she became an elder—if the system lasted that long—she wouldn't perpetuate this kind of inequality. That was assuming she survived today.

She'd only come for a routine digital contact adjustment. The technician had checked her into the exam room and then gone into some back room, leaving her waiting with her thoughts. Beryl heard voices from the adjacent room, muffled but distinct enough for her proximal scanner to enhance.

"—recalibration of the ancient designs—"

"—absolutely essential to keep the seeders in the dark—"

Her heart raced. She had been tracking inconsistencies in official reports for years. Little slip-ups in maintenance logs, odd resource allocations that didn't match stated purposes. Everyone dismissed her theories as paranoia, but she knew better.

She'd just seen the ghost ship with her own eyes, but had nothing to show for it. She needed evidence this time. Something concrete.

With technician still out, Beryl slipped into the bathroom. She pressed her ear against the wall, trying to hear more, when the door opened behind her.

Two figures in pale yellow royal technician uniforms—the same voices she'd heard—looked at her with sudden suspicion.

"Can I help you?" one asked.

"Wrong room," Beryl mumbled, hurrying past them.

She walked away from them for a distance but kept her proximal scanner fixed on their whereabouts. Seeing that they had entered a sealed conference room, she doubled back in their direction. With the corridor empty, she approached the climate control terminal beside the door. She knew these systems were all networked, and might be susceptible to a vulnerability she'd exploited before.

She pulled out her modded access card and tapped it to the reader as she keyed a bypass sequence on the touchpad. The terminal blinked green at her credentials, and began playing the audio happening within the room. Trying to look nonchalant, she brought her ear close to the control's audio output to listen in.

Footsteps from behind her. More than one person.

"I... don't think you're supposed to be doing that." A man's voice. He sounded tired.

The second voice was calm, authoritative. "What's your ID?"

Beryl bolted, careful not to look back so they couldn't identify her, her peripheral vision catching only a flash of security uniform. She ducked around corners, through treatment rooms, and finally stopped behind a supply cabinet to catch her breath.

After a few moments, Beryl's ragged breathing steadied enough for her to hear beyond the hammering of her own heart. She pressed her back against the cabinet's cool metal, and sweat trickled down her spine. No heavy footfalls echoing through the corridors. No security alerts blaring over the comm system. Whoever had caught her hadn't followed.

She allowed herself a shaky exhale, but relief gave way to a new dread. What if they hadn't pursued because they didn't need to? What if they'd simply gone to alert security, who even now might be sealing off sections of the medical ward and scanning for unauthorized access?

Her hand went automatically to her temple where her proximal scanner should be—and found nothing. In her panic, she'd abandoned it at the terminal. They'd surely have confiscated it.

A sharp beep from her wrist panel startled her. The technician was on her way back to the exam room. Should she retrace her steps to retrieve the scanner? Was it worth the risk? That scanner was like an appendage of her body.

No, she'd have to let it go. She couldn't just be seen to have disappeared during her appointment. At this point, it doubled as her alibi. If she arrived late—in a cold sweat, as she was now— they'd suspect she was up to something.

Beryl made her way back to the exam room on unsteady legs. Without her scanner, everything seemed two-dimensional. She couldn't analyze materials or detect surveillance fields or read micro-expressions. She felt naked. She did her best to give off the blank affect she believed normal people wore.

"Are you alright?" the technician asked as Beryl lowered herself into the exam chair. Sweat beaded on her forehead despite the room's perfect temperature control. "You look flushed."

"Just... excited to get my new contacts," she managed.

The technician leaned over Beryl, her gloved fingers steady as she placed the removal tool against Beryl's right eye. A soft suction sound, then the contact lifted away—a gossamer-thin disc of circuitry and synthetic polymer. She repeated the process with the left eye.

"Blink a few times," the technician instructed, setting the contacts in a diagnostic cradle. Blue light swept over the lenses.

Beryl's vision was blurry, the world now very quiet and disconnected without the enhanced overlay she'd grown accustomed to. The technician held up a standard vision chart and checked her baseline acuity while the contacts underwent their scan.

"Hardware has a few bugs," the technician murmured, studying the readout. "Minor calibration drift in the left lens, but I don't think that was what caused the interference you described. I'll have the lab craft your new set, but in the meantime, please wait in the observation area."

Observation. The word sent a chill through her. Did they know? Was this a trap?

In the waiting area, Beryl alternated between sitting rigidly on the edge of her seat and pacing nervous circuits around the room. Without her scanner, she couldn't tell if she was being watched, couldn't detect hidden surveillance.

To her complete dismay, more than once, other patients mistook her for staff, and they asked her annoying questions about medications and therapy schedules. All she could do was smile vaguely and pretend not to hear. Were people really so absentminded as to assume she was staff simply because she wore a light-colored uniform?

The irony of her situation wasn't lost on her. She'd perhaps possibly found evidence of a genuine conspiracy, only to end up in a place where if she said anything, everyone would assume she was paranoid. These people weren't prepared for a revelation.

Her wrist panel showed she'd been waiting three times longer than standard procedure dictated. They might be stalling, or perhaps reviewing security footage, or worse—

they might already be preparing some sort of elaborate "processing" for people who saw too much.

Beryl tried reaching Mott's cabin but there was no answer. She routed it to Mott's personal interface. Still no answer.

More time passed and she felt mealtime hunger gnaw at her empty stomach, a hollow ache that made her lightheaded. For a moment, she decided she'd had enough of this interminable waiting—blurry vision or no, she could find her way to the door and scout for something to eat. But no, she vowed to stay put, and forced herself to sit.

If Mott was already in transit, it was possible she wasn't within range of a comm station. It would explain why Beryl received no confirmation of Mott getting the message.

The uncertainty was worse than the hunger. Were they waiting outside the door, faceless figures in white uniforms ready to apprehend her the moment she stepped out? Or was this simply a normal administrative delay, paperwork being processed somewhere while she sat forgotten in this room filled with confused strangers?

She was realizing just how much she depended on her proximal scanner. How did people get around without knowing everything that happened around them? Normal senses weren't enough for Beryl.

The device was practically an extension of her nervous system. Without it, she felt doubly blind. Every surface and object became a threat or mystery. She couldn't automatically read warning labels or identify materials. She couldn't even be certain of the proper use of the various medical implements arranged on nearby trays.

Which is how she found herself lifting what she thought was a food container to her lips, only to discover—to the barely contained amusement of a passing maintenance crew—that it was actually a dish of datapad cartridges.

Beryl bit back a retort.

A sudden commotion drew everyone's attention. Through the ward's main entrance came a procession of medical staff surrounding what appeared to be an accident victim. Though her vision was blurry, Beryl could make out the telltale signs of radiation burns.

"Another one from the construction site," someone muttered. "Third this week. They really shouldn't let them onto our ward."

MOMENTUM MISDIRECTED

The ore transport would carry us to safety. Just not the safety we needed, not the place we intended, not the future we'd planned.

I watched the asteroid debris drift past our viewport, each chunk of rock, for all I knew, harboring another hidden outpost, another pocket of society's outskirts I'd never known about, despite the fact that this was the very society I was conditioned to love and respect.

The transport cube's automated systems hummed steadily, and we progressed toward what I hoped would be safety. But my mind kept returning to everything we'd just witnessed, and I tried to fit it all into what I thought I knew about my life.

Growing up on the IHC-111, they taught us that everything had its proper place and function. Anything that didn't, well, that should happen only on recdays. The three ships worked in harmony: IHC for the young generation of engineers learning their roles and tending the systems, BZT for the middle generation doing the practical work of keeping us all alive, and PNO for the elders guiding our course.

I watched out the viewport and saw closer than ever before the sheer quantity of debris that our society created from all that was necessary for refueling, repairing, and adding to our raw material stores. These hunks of rocks were precious finds, and our crews clearly did the best they could at harvesting all that they had to offer. It was our right to claim these finds as our own. There was no one else out here, and it was just as likely there would never again be any other human crew in this small corner in the absolute vastness of space.

But seeing the debris made me ponder for the first real time what our legacy would actually be. Maybe this it all we'd ever accomplish. Suppose we were able to succeed at our survival and persist as a three-ship society for many more thousands of years. Should we ever come to a remotely habitable planet, we would finally fulfill our goal. We would seed it with the stuff to generate life, and in time, life would spawn and thrive. But at what cost? Was that truly the picture of success? Is what the final objective of life is? To plunder resources and seek ever to expand? Would that newly seeded life simply set its sights on doing the same?

It would be easy to look at the fields of plundered rocks and blame the renegades or say it was the aesthetic of droids, or to excuse the mass consumption of resources in defense of our mission's importance, but surely there must be some better ambition beyond trying to survive at all costs and expend entire generations of life in the process toward a mission, humanitarian or not.

I sat with my feelings for a few moments in silence. As for us, what was our alternative? We were alone out here. We had no solar warmth to support regenerative cycles. To survive, we needed to move ever onward. The thought of simply letting go was to surrender for no reason, and to doom the previous generations to a charted course that terminated in resignation. They hadn't known the outcome, and neither did I. And I knew it wasn't my fate to ever see it. But I had to believe something better than I could imagine was possible. I supposed we would need to persist until we knew the reason. At least the original seeders had hoped for an end that could justify the means.

I remembered my first maintenance apprenticeship outside the IHC, when I had worked for a brief time alongside a BZT supervisory crew repairing atmospheric processors. They spoke with a sort of respect about the wild potential of these outer reaches. "The PNO can issue all the protocols they want," my supervisor had said, "but out here, you need to understand how things really work."

How did they really work? I still couldn't reconcile how different things were beyond the safe zone surrounding the IHC. Did all these renegades really have no place else to call home? Where did they go when we packed up and kicked the fleet into high speed to the next waypoint?

"You know," I said to the others, "I don't understand how there could be so many of those rogue droids just appearing out of nowhere like that. Why does our society tolerate them? Even better, how can we support such high numbers of them? Someone had to program them, provide them with resources..." I trailed off, thinking about Rono and its strange mix of independence and honor.

"The royal families," Jim finished. "They're playing both sides. Keeping everyone dependent on their protection. I do think they're planning something."

"Jim," I said gently. "Correct me if I'm wrong, but aren't you and Jelini part of the extended royal lines? Your elders certainly are. And yet when you speak of the royals, you sound... reproachful."

Jim made a face. "Hey, we can't help it. We were born this way." He shrugged. "Anyway, until we officially come of age, we're supposed to get treated just like everyone else."

Jelini had been quiet, but now she spoke up. "There's definitely a plan." She tapped the diagram on the back of the datapad, then looked over to me. "Do you think it's on purpose that they keep all of us on the IHC so isolated? So we won't see what's really happening?"

I nodded slowly. "They say it's to protect us, to let us focus on learning. But maybe..." I thought of Beryl, trying to warn us about something she'd discovered. "Maybe they're afraid of what we'd do if we knew the whole truth. Think about it this way—if they didn't believe we could upset their agenda, they wouldn't need to keep us believing that all Smith had to say was 'A clean engine is a happy engine.'"

"All this makes me wonder who we're talking about when we say 'they,'" Jim said. "T7 had known. but what good had that done them?"

"Well, T7 wasn't just one person," Eggi said. "My elder once let slip that it was a whole network—seven founding members who discovered something in the ship's deep archives. They say the seventh member disappeared completely, along with an entire section of records from Year 12. T7's writings always refer to 'the Seven Who Saw' and 'the Six Who Remained.'

The BZT's massive hull filled our viewport now, and I admired how marked its surface was with countless docking ports and repair bays. Somewhere in there were people who might help us understand what we'd stumbled into—if we could reach them before the renegades realized where we'd gone.

The BZT was a rugged industrial giant compared to the mildly pockmarked vessel we called home. Unlike the clean lines and orderly compartments of the IHC, this ship wore its function openly. Mining equipment and processing modules protruded from its hull like organs exposed beneath torn skin. Extraction cranes jutted from reinforced docking bays, some still clutching asteroid fragments. This was mining itself in all its functional beauty.

I thought about Superior Smith's hidden writings, about foundations built by rebels rather than rulers. Maybe it was time for another kind of rebellion, but this one of truth.

The hum of the transport cube shifted in tone. The loading systems operated on the principle that everything had to be sorted, tagged, and properly routed. Right now, the transport cube was running through its pre-delivery sequence.

A mechanical arm swung down from the ceiling and its sensors scanned the cube. The control panel's placid green indicator light changed to orange and started blinking. Text spawned on the display.

"BIOLOGICAL CONTAMINATION DETECTED. INITIATING QUARANTINE PROTOCOL."

"Contamination on the cube? Yuck!" Jelini said. "I sure hope they're able to get rid of it."

From each side of us, a nickel-iron containment field began to fold in around us, ready to enclose us within a solid metal cube.

"No, I think the scanner's registering us as biological contaminants," I said. "This transport is designed for ore and droids, not humans. The system thinks we're some kind of infection."

The screen blinked again: "DECONTAMINATION SEQUENCE INITIATING IN THIRTY SECONDS."

Jim pounded against the cube's walls. "There has to be an override!"

I ran my hands over the interior surface, looking for any kind of control panel or emergency release.

"These containers aren't designed for living cargo," Eggi said, his voice tight with dawning realization. "There are no manual controls inside because droids would communicate wirelessly with the system."

"Mott, do you know what happens during decontamination?" Jelini asked, her eyes wide.

I couldn't find my breath. "High-temp flash plasma sterilization. It would... it would vaporize any organic material."

In the distance beyond the walls on their way to enclose us, I could see the automated loading systems preparing to receive us. No human operators in sight.

"We need to get someone's attention," Jim said, kicking at the walls.

"DECONTAMINATION IN TWENTY SECONDS."

"Eggi, you're right. The comms!" I pulled at my suit collar and extracted a thin filament.

Beneath the panel was a systems aggregation array joining it to the master subpanel. I didn't need to send a message. All I needed to do was cause a short in one of the systems.

I yanked a connector free and used my spare filament to bridge it across two junction points. The panel sparked and popped. A cascade of error signals streamed through the transport's systems.

A moment later, the main communication array lit up like a festival display, and it broadcast the cube's error code to the docking station's receiver.

"DECONTAMINATION IN TEN SECONDS."

"There's no one listening!" Jim shouted.

"Someone has to be monitoring these systems," I insisted, my eyes scanning the docking bay beyond our prison. "The BZT wouldn't run entirely on automation. And even if it were automated, it should register this as—"

"FIVE. FOUR. THREE."

A sharp crackle of static burst through our panic.

"SYSTEM OVERRIDE ENGAGED," the automated voice announced in the same measured tone. "QUARANTINE PROTOCOL SUSPENDED. AWAITING FURTHER INSTRUCTIONS."

The containment field remained where it was, nearly enclosing us. With a jarring thud, the arm dropped our cube onto the loading dock floor. Metal clamps slammed shut around us and secured our vessel in place.

Two workers hurried over. One held a radio to her mouth murmuring instructions, and the other kept a standard-issue blaster in low ready position, finger resting near the trigger guard.

"It's kids," the first worker said with disbelief, lowering her radio. "You aren't supposed to use these things for transports." She gestured at our improvised vehicle as if its unsuitability was the most obvious thing in the universe. "They're calibrated to sterilize anything biological that isn't properly registered."

"That's a good point you make," I said, stepping out into the blessed open space of the docking bay. "We'll remember that for next time."

The worker holstered the gun. "What the hell do you IHC kids think you're doing?" His face gave nothing away, but his tone didn't seem to be genuinely concerned.

Jelini stepped forward and clasped her hands behind her back, tilting her head to make it clear to any observer that she was adorably innocent and that was all.

"If you only knew what we'd just escaped, you would know we're not trying to cause any trouble," she said, her voice sweet as honey. "Adaptability is a virtue, isn't that what they teach us?"

I couldn't match her poise. The words tumbled out of me in a desperate rush. "We need to speak to security immediately! Our ship—a Freyan-class shuttle—it was stolen by renegade droids and we barely escaped with our lives!"

The workers exchanged glances. The one with the gun let out a barking laugh.

"Oh sure, right, kid," he said, holstering the weapon. "I'm sure security will be fascinated by your little adventure story."

"How dare you insinuate that we're lying!" I protested, feeling heat rise in my cheeks. "Mudar and Crasp could be after us right now! They have our ship, and it's not just some junkcraft—it's a Freyan cruiser!"

The worker stared at us for a moment. "I don't think you have a clue how offensive that 'renegade' talk is. Haven't you learned anything about droid rights in your fancy classes? I think you having access to that Freyan cruiser must be distracting you from your studies."

"How do you kids think we get so much done during our resource gathering stops? Droids have their own ways of handling things. Sounds to me like you all have yourselves to blame."

"Take that transit pod to central hub," the other worker said, pointing vaguely to our left, already turning away. "Security station's on level four. They'll get you sorted and back to IHC where you belong."

As they walked away, their muttered conversation drifted back to us.

"Renegade droids, my ass."

"'Boobar and Cress could be after us right now!'" the other chuckled. "Back when we used to pull that kind of stuff, we at least sounded more convincing."

The first worker called at us over their shoulder. "Word of warning—you're in a droid zone of the BZT. Some of our mechanical equals have attitudes, but they keep this place running. Show some respect, yeah? Things are tense enough between organics and mechanicals these days."

I watched them go, my shoulders slumping. How had everything changed so much? Each time I'd visited the BZT in the past, droids had been tools, not equals—certainly not beings about which it was inconceivable to accuse of wrongdoing.

We headed toward the transit pod they'd indicated. In the distance, I could see several droids going about their business. They moved with a swagger. A few of them had modified their chassis with decorative elements, statements of individuality.

The BZT I remembered from my apprenticeship only a few years prior had been orderly, hierarchical, with clear chains of command. This place felt more lawless by comparison. Ironic to have a feeling of lawlessness when surrounded by beings of computational excess. But clearly the station's power dynamics had shifted in ways I couldn't quite grasp.

We boarded the transport train that snaked through the BZT's central corridor, a chain of linked pods with transparent walls that offered unforgiving visibility in all directions. Through the viewport to our left, I watched the massive processing equipment recede as we accelerated, while the window on our right revealed only darkness punctuated by occasional maintenance lights. Most unsettling were the clear partitions between each car which eliminated any illusion of privacy from fellow passengers or the watchful eyes of other droids. I reminded myself that we had been victims of a series of accidents, that we had nothing to hide, and even more, that we were among allies.

My nerves jangled with each gentle sway of the pod. If we were spotted now by Mudar and Crasp, there'd be nowhere to run. It was just smooth, sealed walls and the gaping void of space beyond. I scanned the faces of my young companions and hoped they comprehended how precarious our situation still was. One wrong word, one suspicious glance from another passenger, and we might find ourselves detained, separated, subjected to some droid collective's idea of retribution. I couldn't let that happen to them. Not after everything we'd already survived.

Through the viewport to the next pod, movement caught my eye. Two droids stood facing each other, their gestures becoming increasingly agitated. Before long, what had begun as staring and subtle posturing escalated and became more aggressive.

"Maybe a trading dispute," Eggi whispered, seeing the scene. "If these are independent merchants, I would imagine some are in charge of valuable cargo. And from what I gather about droids, they seem every bit as adversarial as humans."

I found myself nodding in agreement.

One droid was sleek and polished, with ornate gold filigree glyphs worked into its chassis, like tattoos showing off of some of its signature code. Most likely customized from a base model vendor unit, the intent was clearly to convey a touch of class.

The second was built from the base model of a Scrounger. It was bulkier and more utilitarian, and looked cobbled together from mismatched parts. While less refined than the vendor, it had a sturdy, practical design. Its weapons were obvious—exposed gun barrels and flame units welded directly to its frame.

In no time, the vendor had the scrounger pinned against a wall with two of its arms, and was striking at it. The hits came in rapid succession. After a few hits, some pieces got knocked off from its adversary. If I were to guess, I would have said that the rapid blows were meant as a distraction, because with its central arm the vendor made attempts to grasp, rip, and punch at its opponent's central processing unit.

They fought and they dodged and they fought some more. Despite the brutality the vendor was able to inflict on the scrounger unit, the whole attack looked like something that could go on for a very long time. When a piece or limb was knocked off, the severed limb socket quickly sprouted metal mesh tendrils that writhed and groped for the missing limb until at last they made contact with it. Within seconds, what had been dismembered components had been reassembled once more into deadly weapons. Even debris from the assault—sheared bolts and bits of reinforcing steel skin that fell to the ground were in time reabsorbed back into the droid through some mysterious intake port near the base. Although its autorepair capability was truly impressive, something I'd only read about before, the violence was cold, calculated, and somehow felt worse than any human brawl I'd ever witnessed.

I'd seen enough. All my life aboard the IHC-111, there had been a life built on a foundation of respect. Peace. Even if it felt constraining, at least it prevented this kind of senseless brutality. Even though these were just machines, I couldn't bear the sight of it. Someone needed to step in, and since none of the other passengers wanted anything to do with the melee, I supposed it needed to be me.

I pressed the button on the inter-pod comm. "Stop!" I shouted. "I don't know what you two are fighting over, but it can't be worth that. Stop this fighting!"

To my dismay, the droids paused their combat, and their optical sensors swiveled to focus on us. The scrapper spoke first, its voice carrying the harmonics of a Mark VI merchant, "Well, well. What have we here? Some lost little biologicals from an IHC field trip?"

As it spoke, the two of them in unison began heading toward us. I reached to secure the door between pods, but it had no lock.

"Look at their clothes," the vendor droid added. "Maintenance workers. Probably don't even have proper neural interfaces." Its vocabulator produced something like a laugh. "How primitive."

I felt my face flush with anger, but before I could respond, Jim stepped forward and spoke into the comm. "By the Proverbs of Superior Smith," he declared, his voice steady, "strength flows not from the capacity to destroy, but from the wisdom to preserve."

The droids' reaction might have been comical under other circumstances. Their optical sensors widened, and their servos whirred as they parsed the sincerity of this unexpected proclamation. As they approached the connecting door, it slid open and they stepped through into our pod. The old man at the opposite end of our pod sat undisturbed, and continued reading his datapad as before.

The vendor droid eyed Jim. "You say pretty words, biological. Let's see how they hold up against—"

I raised my hands and stood in front of Jim, in between us and the two robots. "Stop! Please! We're just passing through. We don't want any trouble."

What happened next happened all at once. From a small tube in what we'd call the droid's neck, the vendor droid fired a small, spherical device that headed rapidly toward Jim. I dove toward the projectile so that it would hit me instead, but it dodged me and arced around to attach itself splat in the middle of Eggi's face. A mercurial black goo spread over his cheek, nose, mouth and eye. The goo revealed itself to be some type of nanopaste. What first appeared to be a mere puddle began to organize and structure itself, tiny organic circuits and transistors spreading across his skin.

"Boosterbot swarm!" Jelini screamed.

Boosterbots were metallic self-replicating nanites that droids used to recover from structural damage—their artificial immune system.

Now those same nanites crawled across Eggi's skin seeking vulnerabilities and probing for entry points. I'd heard stories of maintenance workers who'd accidentally triggered the release of active boosterbots and not gotten prompt medical attention—their flesh gradually transformed into something neither fully organic nor truly mechanical.

If we didn't get them off him soon, Eggi would be fundamentally altered, perhaps forever.

I lunged at the vendor droid, grabbing its prized central weapon arm and twisting. The limb came off, metal connectors snapping as it separated from the core shoulder socket. Inside the exposed joint, I spotted what I had hoped to find: a universal remote actuator nestled among the severed wires and hydraulic lines, the control device used during construction and maintenance, which was by design intended to be left secured inside the unit. I pried open its protective panel, overloaded the dial so that it would work against multiple units, aimed it at the two droids and pressed the yellow suspension button. Their movements slowed then froze entirely. Their optical sensors glowing, their limbs were locked in position.

"Don't you even try a thing," I growled, "or I'll shut you both down permanently."

The droids were motionless, their combat routines inert, the silvery metal mesh command nexus in the arm socket extending outward to find the arm to reattach it, but could not reach to where I held it.

Jelini used the sleeve of her shirt to help Eggi brush off the excess nanites.

The old man at the end of the pod finally looked up from his datapad, muttered something that sounded like "tourists," and went back to reading.

I heard a faint high-pitched whine. In the next instant, I saw the Scrapper droid's chest cannon begin to charge. Clearly, it tapped into some inner reserves and was finding a workaround. Once charged, it would be ready to fire point-blank at me.

Tossing the severed arm of the Vendor to Jim, I launched myself at the second droid, grabbing its head with both hands. Years of maintenance work had taught me a good deal about where to find the emergency release catches on robotic equipment. The head came free with a spray of hydraulic fluid and streams of sparks.

Its body stood where it was, dumb and inert, while the Vendor, somehow, made the slightest of movements.

Jim pointed the remote actuator at the remaining droid, his hand shaking but his aim true. "Stand down. Now."

I heard the hiss of the pod arriving at its next location.

"This is a violation of machine rights," the Vendor's muffled voice protested.

"This is a violation of my face", Eggi said.

"The old order is ending," the droid warned. "Soon, biological life will—"

"Save it," I cut him off. "We're leaving. And if you try to follow us..." I hefted the heavy droid head in my hands and elbowed Jim. Jim, prompted, waved the hand menacingly.

The Vendor made no reply. We backed out of the pod carefully, and just before the door hissed closed, Jim and I tossed the head and arm back into the car so the droid could repair his friend or enemy, I still wasn't clear which.

THE WRONG SALVATION

In which the BZT proves less hostile in unexpected ways.

Only when the pod whirred away did I let myself breathe normally again. "Eggi, are you alright?"

He nodded, rubbing his face.

"The swarm," Jelini pointed at Eggi's face. "It's growing."

She was right. The tiny machines had stopped their random spread and were now arranging themselves into something more like circuit pathways.

"We've got to get you to a clinic," Jelini said.

"Actually, there's a Droid Repair shop not far away," I said, remembering the layout of this section of the BZT. "It's close, and if it's what I think it is, they'll have the right kind of equipment to remove the infestation." The logic was questionable, taking a human to a robotic repair facility. But surely they would be equipped to handle the basic spectrum of human-robot ailments.

We fled through the docking bay, dodging around startled crew members and automated cargo handlers.

The repair ward was three decks down in a section of the ship dedicated to maintenance and processing. The corridors here were wider, designed to accommodate larger mechanical units, and the lighting had a distinct bluish tint that was supposed to help with precision work.

"Through here," I directed, leading them through a set of heavy doors marked 'Mechanical Rehabilitation Center.' Everything was metal and composite materials, with equipment more like industrial machinery than tools of healing.

A spindly repair droid approached us, its optical sensors adjusting to take in the strange sight of four humans in its domain. "State the nature of the malfunction," it requested in a staccato monotone voice.

"Our friend," I gestured to Eggi, trying not to sound as terrified as I was, "was exposed to what I think is at least a third generation gram positive boosterbot swarm."

The droid's processors whirred as it analyzed this information. "Please proceed to Diagnostic Bay 7. This unit will alert Head Mechanic HookNode Pless."

They led Eggi to a repair cradle—basically a metallic grate surrounded by articulated arms holding various tools and scanners. He lay back, trying to look brave despite the obvious fear in his eyes.

"You're doing great," I assured him. "This is exactly the kind of thing they're equipped to handle. It probably happens all the time."

Jim and Jelini huddled nearby as the equipment began its work, scanning the patterns on Eggi's face.

We were directed to wait in a small adjacent room while they performed the procedure. The space was clearly designed for droids awaiting repairs—all hard angles and charging stations instead of comfortable seating.

After what felt like hours but was probably only minutes, a larger droid entered—presumably HookNode Pless. Its frame was decorated with various achievements and certification markers. Its movements were slow and precise, clearly those of a technician who took themselves very seriously.

"Oh my," it said, its vocabulator modulating tones of concern. "Your friend is the biological?"

"Yes," I replied, impatience creeping into my voice. "Is he..."

"Oh, I'm very sorry," Pless interrupted, its optical sensors dimming in what seemed like genuine regret. "That unit was sent to the sterilization ward. Grew eyes all over its body. Such optic capacity a biological can hardly endure for long. Its last moments were full of excruciating pain, but it's completely deactivated now."

My heart stopped. Jim grabbed my arm. Jelini made a small, choked sound.

"What?" I managed to gasp. "It was only a bit of nanobots."

"Oh!" The droid's sensors brightened. "My apologies. I was referring to the batch of quasi-organic space lichen we processed earlier. Easy to confuse between two biologicals. You all look alike to us." It made a sound that might have been meant as a chuckle. "Your friend is fine. The boosterbot swarm was successfully contained and neutralized. Though I must say, his cells showed remarkable readiness to evolve into a superior life form, which is to say a droid. We don't often see organics handle mechanical integration so well."

Relief flooded through me, followed quickly by annoyance at the droid's casual equation of humans with fungal growth. But before I could say anything, Pless continued.

"Though I must note—seeking treatment in a mechanical facility rather than a biological medical ward is. . . unusual. One might even say inspiring."

I wasn't sure, but it seemed like the droid-doctor winked at me.

"However, this unit's primary directive is repair and restoration. Questions of allegiance and protocol are, shall we say, secondary concerns." It turned toward the viewport where we could now see Eggi sitting up, the angry patterns on his face already fading. "Your friend will make a full recovery. The swarm's repair protocols have been fully neutralized. Perhaps unfortunately."

"Thank you," I said, meaning it, but also very ready to put this phase of our adventure behind us.

"Pause one moment," Pless interrupted. "There is the matter of payment. You are aware this is not a Company hospital."

I froze, also cognizant that my pockets did not hold any credits.

But Pless continued: "We of course also consider barters such as data exchange as payment. Perhaps..." It waved its arm suggestively.

I thought of the crystal I'd gotten from Jelini back in Mudar's office. I had a vague sense that it might have some value, and had no idea what use it could be to me otherwise.

"Deal," I said, pulling out the crystal.

"Centaurian oracle crystal, excellent." As the droid's manipulators carefully took the crystal, it added casually, "I'll see to it this ward also removes all records of your visit from the central database. Mechanical precision requires... selective memory, at times."

The door to the treatment room opened and Eggi joined us in the hallway, looking shaken but intact. The boosterbot wound had faded to barely visible lines that could easily be explained as simple irritation.

"How do you feel?" Jelini asked him.

"Like I got hit in the face with a swarm of illegal auto-repairing robots," he replied with a smile. "But otherwise okay."

"Fascinating response to the integration," Pless mused, studying Eggi with renewed interest. "Most impressive for a biological. When the great improvement takes place, you may make the cut."

That comment sent a chill down my spine.

"We should go," I said firmly. "Beryl's still waiting for us."

That's when we rounded a corner and nearly collided with a familiar stack of rotating bronze discs.

"Rono?" I blurted, surprised to see the droid here.

The merchant droid was reclined in some sort of very high-end maintenance station jutting into the hallway, some of its disc segments partially disassembled while repair arms worked on its internal mechanisms. The blue energy fields between its sections flickered intermittently.

"Ah, the troublesome biologicals," Rono's liquid-metal voice carried a note of amusement. "I was wondering when you'd turn up."

The repair station Rono occupied was clearly reserved for premium clients—the equipment probably cost more than most junkcraft. Several of Rono's disc segments were suspended in null-gravity fields while tiny welding arms worked on their edges.

It wasn't until that point that I had noticed Rono's previously sulfuric smell had largely gone away. Perhaps it was whatever new equipment he'd had patched on during the repairs—the hearty acrid smell of newly forged alloys against a base of its familiar copper and synthfruit, the soldered wafts from newly heated circuits and fresh welding. The scent reminded me of the IHC's engine room after a major overhaul, when new components were still settling in, their materials off-gassing as they integrated with existing systems. It made my nose tingle and the hair on the back of my neck stand on end.

The repair arms continued their work applying microsealant to the droid's disc edges. Each sealed segment glowed with an inner light before settling back to its normal bronze sheen. The blue energy fields between the segments looked more stable now, their color deeper and more uniform. Rono was clearly getting more than just basic repairs. This was a full upgrade, the kind that would cost a fortune in synthpacks.

"Glad you made it to safety. Is your ship all right?" Jim asked.

"Protecting your escape came with some structural costs," Rono replied. "You owe me several synthpacks."

"*Several* synthpacks?" I felt my heart sink. The synthetic power units were the preferred currency out in the belt, and they incremented in units well beyond what anyone I knew aboard the IHC-111 ever dealt with. Back at home, we more or less got by on a few credits here and there. We had our basic needs accounted for, and anything extra came from putting in a proportional amount of hard work. No one I knew had more than a dozen credits to their name, and it was around a hundred credits for each synthpack. Needless to say, I couldn't produce a single one, let alone several. "I'd love to help you out, Rono, but I just can't afford that."

"Once again, your biology misleads you. The payment is not for these repairs," Rono interrupted, gesturing at its current maintenance work. "And not for my ship. It's for yours. I'm asking that you pay for the repairs to your ship."

"Our ship?"

"The Maltan vessel. I had a—let's call it a discussion—with Hannick. I don't think you've seen the last of her. I managed to renegotiate ownership. But getting it rushed into Astero's Salvage required... significant resource expenditure. Several of my best silicon stashes."

The droid's optical sensor fixed on me. "I stuck my neck out for you—figuratively speaking, of course—so don't leave me hanging." A pause. "Figuratively speaking."

Rono's generosity suprised me, and I didn't know what to say. I felt the others looking to me for direction. The Maltan's ship was our ticket home—if we could get it repaired. But we had no synthpacks.

Jelini reached into her pockets and produced the data crystals she'd nabbed from Crasp's office. They caught the dim light as she held them out.

Rono's optical sensor focused on the offering, its aperture widening then narrowing in quick assessment. The droid's central discs rotated slightly—a mechanical approximation of a head shake.

"Interesting," Rono's metallic voice carried a hint of genuine curiosity. "Undoubtedly interesting finds."

The droid's manipulator reached out, hovering over the crystals without taking them. A small vent on what might be considered Rono's throat emitted a burst of static-laden sound—something between a broadcast error and deliberate vocalization.

"But those in total wouldn't amount to a percentage of the sum I'm needing here," Rono added, the manipulator withdrawing. The sound repeated, louder this time, unmistakably a mechanical approximation of scoffing dismissal.

"OK, we can't pay now, but maybe we could work out some kind of—"

"You're in no position for haggling." The droid's tone was final. "The economics of the belt are precarious enough without extending credit to. . ." a slight whir of processors, "unauthorized borrowers of Freyan-class shuttles."

"But it was an emergency, and it's still an emergency. Now it's even more of an emergency!" Jelini interjected.

"Perhaps," Rono mused as repair arms reattached one of its segments, "It's time for you take this as a lesson in the true nature of independence. Out here, everything has a price. Even freedom."

I wanted to argue, but the droid was right. We'd jumped into this mission without resources, without a backup plan, and now we were paying the price. It was a miracle that the

Maltan's ship would be repaired eventually, but that didn't help us now.

I wondered if a dose of emotional sugar worked on droids. "Thank you," I said, and I meant it despite everything. "For helping us escape. And for saving the ship."

Rono's discs rotated in acknowledgment. "Gratitude is appreciated but again unacceptable as a substitute form of payment. Gratitude does not provide plasma fuel to the ion accelerators, as they say."

There would be no arguing with the droid. I started to turn away.

"We'll have to owe you. Where is the ship now?"

The droid's optical sensor dimmed briefly, then brightened. "Yes, you still owe me for the tow, but I'd rather have you owe me. Favors are more valuable than synthpacks in many cases. I left the ship at Astero's, where it's being repaired. How you work out payment for the actual repairs is between you and Astero."

The repair arms finished their work, and Rono's segments locked back into formation.

It was a step forward in our quest, but also a new obstacle. Everything about this day was bigger than I'd bargained for. The renegades, the royal plots, the strange ship—all of it stretched beyond my understanding of what our society truly was. Standing there in the repair ward, I studied this droid who had both endangered and saved us, and I nodded in acknowledgment.

We continued down the hallway and exited the repair ward on the most direct path toward the intership transport zone, which led us through the ship's heavily industrial middle section.

The main security desk for this zone would be right down this hall, but as we made our way there, something didn't feel right. The thought nagged at me that if we went and tried to talk to the authorities, we'd be walking into a trap. Hadn't everything so far been a curve ball here, on a much bigger and more complicated society than I'd ever envisioned?

And if I merely took the supposedly responsible path—was that actually the childish thing? To run to security—to adults—when things got hard? They'd just do what everyone else had done: try to control the situation, be overbearing, take over. Once I put things in their hands, it would be game over. My adventure would become their incident report.

So if we didn't throw ourselves at the mercy of the law, where did that leave us? We could try and convince the intership operators to let us travel to the PNO. Perhaps they'd accept a bribe or a clever story. Jelini seemed to have a special skill with those things.

Running into Rono had been a strange grace. We didn't need security oversight. We needed our ship back. Maybe the real adult approach was to take ownership and make good the path I'd chosen, however rough it had gotten. I didn't like how that felt, but it felt like the right thing to do.

I couldn't make this decision alone, though. I needed to talk it over with the others. Whatever we did next, I needed their buy-in. We were in this together now.

And what a strange place we had come to. Heat radiated from massive processing units that stretched three decks high, their surfaces scarred by decades of constant operation. The air itself felt different—thicker, laden with metallic particles and the spirity smell of industrial solvents that someone like me paradoxically found satisfying, although not exactly health-bestowing.

Workers moved to and fro with the inscrutable faces of the middle generation. No training supervisors here, no educational simulations—just the relentless rhythm of actual work that processed ore and generated the raw materials that kept our fleet alive.

When we had come at last to a quiet hallway, I pulled everyone into an alcove.

"Listen," I said, meeting each of their eyes in turn. "I've been making decisions without consulting you, and that stops now."

Jim raised an eyebrow. Eggi's mouth twitched into the beginning of a smile.

"The truth is," I continued, "you've all shown more skill and intelligence today than I expected. Than I gave you credit for." I swallowed hard. "In many ways, more than I have."

Jelini nodded seriously, as if she knew all along that I would say this. I was starting to see what Jim found annoying.

"So I'm asking—what you think we should do next? Beryl's still waiting, possibly in danger, and we're stranded without a ship." I spread my hands. "The distance between the BZT and PNO is vast, but people make the journey all the time. We have no official clearance, which means if we try and gain passage through the official channels, they'll insist on sending us back to the IHC, but there has to be a way."

I continued. "The right thing to do is probably talk to security. It's why we came this way in the first place." My voice sounded hollow even to me. I knew what the proper procedure was—report the incident, let the authorities handle it. That's what responsible people did. But a knot formed in my stomach as I thought about surrendering our agency to them. "We were wronged out there. Security should believe us, take our side, help us out."

I paused, feeling the weight of my next words. "But if we involve them, we can't make the decision for them. And whatever they say, they'll make us do." The thought of being forced back to the IHC, of Beryl left alone waiting for us, of abandoning the shuttle, made my chest tighten.

"On the other hand," I said, voice dropping lower, "our ship is somewhere nearby. We might be able to reclaim it." I didn't need to spell out what that meant—more danger, more rules broken, more responsibility on my shoulders. I looked at their faces, these young clones who'd already risked so much. "That option is maybe the most reckless of all."

The silence that followed was filled with a new kind of respect flowing between us. We weren't just a maintenance worker and three kids anymore. We were a team.

Eggi cleared his throat, and I realized I was genuinely eager to hear what he had to say.

"As I see it," Eggi started in, "Talking to security is unthinkable. Even if they understand that renegades attacked us, they won't believe us for a minute that we had any right to be out there. They'll think that we were up to no good, and maybe they're not wrong about that. So we really only have two options, both of them dangerous, and both of them terrible, which is why I believe that I'm probably on the right track." He gave a charmer's smile. "We could go get the ship, and maybe even wait around there at the garage while it's being repaired, and maybe just steal it once the time came. The other option is to take the next public transport to the PNO, which would entail spoofing our IDs so there's a plausable reason why four youths had a reason to travel there."

I smiled despite myself. Although I didn't like to consider that I was being a very bad influence on them, Eggi's suggestion once more proved to me that these kids were more worldly in many ways than I was, and less bothered by adherence to rules. I could see that the brief time we'd spent together had brought us all closer. Somehow, the experience hadn't dampened their spirits.

Which gave me an idea.

MASKS AT THE GATHERING

At a party, surrounded by the young and privileged, synthmead flows more freely than wisdom.

The four of us huddled around a systems display I'd managed to access using my maintenance credentials. The holographic map cast a soft blue glow over our faces as we tried to figure out our position in relation to everything else.

"We're here," I pointed to a blinking dot in what was labeled as Processing Zone Alpha-7. I zoomed the map out so that the processing station became a small dot in the distance from a large cigar-shaped vessel. "And we need to get here," I pointed to a section on the PNO's lower decks.

I zoomed back in to the processing station. Multiple docking bays large enough to accommodate industrial vessels. Ore processing substations that could handle tons of raw material per hour. A fully equipped droid hospital facility, which we were already familiar with.

"This," I said, finding my target on the map. "Do you notice anything interesting about that section?"

Jelini squinted her eyes and adjusted the display, zooming in on the area I'd indicated. The label appeared: "School of Ore."

"A training facility," Jim breathed, either understanding immediately or giving the impression that he liked something about the idea. "Where they teach new technicians about mineral processing."

I nodded. "Which means they're used to seeing younger faces. Students. Apprentices."

"Student areas will be access controlled for security purposes. But we don't have any documentation," Jim pointed out. "No student IDs, no classroom clearance, and only the junior techworker clothes we have on us..."

I studied the facility's layout more carefully. The School of Ore occupied several levels, and was connected to both the processing areas and the droid hospital wing. More importantly, it had its own internal transport system to move students between practical training areas.

"Look here," I highlighted a particular route. "The hospital wing where we just were is connected directly to the school's practical medicine lab. For teaching medical staff about industrial accidents and exposure cases."

"But Beryl's not in that hospital," Jelini said, her eyes narrowing. "What am I missing?"

"We won't look out of place if we're dressed like students," I continued. "And the school's interdepartmental transport system..."

"Could get us most of the way there," Eggi finished. "But how do we get student IDs... or otherwise just steal one of those transports?"

"We don't steal things, we borrow them," I retorted, more or less automatically at this point. "Actually, if my plan works, I don't think we'll need to do anything of the sort."

I zoomed in on another section of the map, a small administrative office near our current position. "Every facility like this keeps spare student documentation on hand. For temporary visitors, special courses, that sort of thing."

"Oh, so we're stealing student IDs?" Jim asked, though his tone suggested he was more impressed than concerned.

"Borrowing," I corrected. "We're just borrowing them. Like the ship."

Jelini giggled, then quickly covered her mouth. "Sorry. It's just... we're going to break all these rules and go places where we shouldn't be going just to rescue someone who probably broke into someplace where she shouldn't have been in the first place..." she trailed off, shaking her head.

"We can't abandon Beryl. Whatever happened to her, she clearly is in the middle of something dangerous. Even if we did just go home and pretend nothing happened, your elders will be missing a ship. At this point... we just have to make it work." I pointed out. "You all said you were here for an adventure. So are you with me?"

Resolute nods from Jim, Jelini, and Eggi. The map continued to rotate slowly in the air between us, the School of Ore's layout now more like an opportunity.

"Eggi?" I turned to our resident systems expert. "Think you can handle their registration system?"

Eggi's eyes were already studying the holographic display, analyzing the security architecture. "It's a standard Half-Helix-7 enrollment system. Pretty basic stuff. The real challenge will be the timing. Registration offices always have staff present."

"Not always," Jim corrected, pointing to a schedule overlay. "Look, they're running on reduced staffing because of some special event. Something called..."

I zoomed in on the notification: "Annual Mineral Classification Symposium. All Students Required to Attend."

"That's a wrench in our plans," I breathed. "There's no chance of sneaking through unseen. Everyone will be at the symposium, probably arguing about how to catalog ore samples. We'll stand out like a rusty bolt in spring pudding."

"Or," Jelini's eyes lit up, "we could attend. What better cover than being right where everyone expects students to be? Maybe we happen to be a band of young geniuses with a gift for minerals, and we enrolled younger than most."

She had a point. We had no chance of remaining unseen, but certainly a chance of passing through unnoticed. Sometimes the best way to hide was in plain sight. And a symposium meant crowds, distractions, opportunities...

"Actually," I said slowly, "that might work even better. At an event like that, they'll expect to see unfamiliar faces. Visiting students, guest speakers, or talented young mineral savants like us."

Jelini was studying another part of the map intently. "There's something else. The school uniform specifications..." She highlighted a section showing standard student attire. "These are stored in fabrication units right near the registration office. We could print what we need."

"And if something goes wrong with our plan?" Jim asked.

"Then we do what students do best," I replied with confidence. "We make excuses and run."

They nodded. We were about to attempt something either brilliant or incredibly stupid.

We made our way to the School of Ore's registration wing, but as we approached, something was clearly different from what we'd expected. Instead of the quiet administrative space shown on the maps, the hallways were alive with noise and movement. Music pulsed through the deck plates, and crowds of people in elaborate costumes filled every available space.

"What's happening?" Jelini whispered as we pressed ourselves against a wall to avoid a group wearing what appeared to be ceremonial mining suits. The suits were ridiculously impractical, covered in crystalline formations and metallic embellishments that would never survive actual mining work. Some wore helmets topped with elaborate mineral specimens, while others had incorporated glowing ore samples into complicated headdresses.

"It's not just a symposium," Eggi realized, reading an announcement poster. "It's a costume party too. 'In celebration of our mineral heritage and future innovations in ore processing.'"

"Perfect," I breathed. "No one will look twice at a few oddly-dressed students. Everyone's trying to stand out."

Through the crowd, I could see the registration office— and more importantly, the fabrication units nearby. But reaching them meant navigating through what had essentially become a festival space. Clusters of people gathered around gaming consoles set up in a back room, while others engaged in enthusiastic debates about mineral classification systems.

The music thrummed through the deck plates, and the air was thick with the smell of synthmead and the faint melted-glass odors of fresh-printed hyperfabric. Despite our lack of costumes, the general chaos was proving to be an effective camoflage. Everyone was too busy showing off their own outfits or arguing about mineralogical theory to pay much attention to a few more young faces in the crowd.

"Who'd have ever believed that the Mineral Classification Symposium was a celebration?" Eggi remarked, watching a pair of students drift past in virtualized costumes that made them look like floating molecular structures. "Although I can't say it's really my scene, I do feel like mingling while you all head over to Registration to pick up the uniforms."

"Yeah, we should split up," Jim suggested slyly, his eyes fixed on a doorway where people were gathering around some kind of gaming setup. "Cover more ground, look for the office."

I wasn't having it. "We're here to grab IDs and be on our way. No funny business!"

Like it or not, funny business was definitely an active element at the symposium. The virtualization costumes were constructed from millions of tiny programmed nanites that hovered around the wearer, creating shimmering three-dimensional displays that were less realistic than they were dazzling. Unlike the dangerous boosterbot swarm that had attacked Eqqi earlier, these were purely cosmetic—they could create striking visual effects but not integrate with biological systems.

Music thumped through hidden speakers as more costumed revelers passed us. I spotted outfits themed after famous mineral compositions, historical mining incidents, and even a few people dressed as Superior Smith herself, though each version looked completely different from the others.

We made our way through the crowds, and dodged past a group engaged in a heated debate about prudency of standard versus ancient imperial classification methods. The standard method focused purely on crystalline structure and molecular bonds, nice and orderly, everything in its proper point in the Cartesian myth that described space as a three-dimensional matrix. The imperial method, developed during the early days of space mining and largely abandoned except by iron traders, took into account practical elements like extraction difficulty, refinery requirements, and even the psychological effects of long-term exposure to the model itself on the thought patterns of the mining crews. One student, gesturing dramatically, was insisting that the ancients understood that minerals weren't just raw materials, but had their own kind of animistic volition toward becoming refined, each in its own time, yearning to become alloys and high-grade construction materials. His opponent, wearing a costume that made her look like a walking spectrographic analysis, countered that such "Smithical thinking" had no place in modern ore processing. The real debate, she argued, should be about whether their classification methods were actually serving the practical needs of the seeder fleet, or just maintaining traditions that no longer made sense.

"Both wrong," declaimed a third student, her costume projecting a holographic overlay of Fourier transformations that oscillated into and out of various octaves of harmony. "The real question.. the *real* question.. is how we measure the metrics themselves. Are we even *calculating* mineral value correctly? The whole *system* needs to be rebuilt from the ground up." She, it was easy to see, was the most inebriated of them all.

The argument showed no signs of reaching a conclusion, but had drawn an increasingly passionate crowd.

I looked over at my young clone companions, pointing to the debaters. "And that's why it's good to only drink in moderation."

I noticed Jim's attention still on the console gaming area in the back room, where students were playing some kind of virtual reality simulation. Jelini had become fascinated by a group performing what appeared to be mineral-themed interpretive dance, their virtualized costumes creating trails of crystalline light as they moved. Even Eggi, despite his earlier ordeal, was edging toward a cluster of hip older students.

The responsibility of trying to keep them all together, focused, and safe was starting to wear on me, and I reassessed my sternness. They'd been remarkably resilient through everything we'd faced, and, after all, they were young clones who deserved to let their hair down a little. This was supposed to be their recday too.

"Look," I said, gathering them close. "The registration office is right there. Why don't you three take a break while I handle the documentation? Just... stay in this general area, and try not to draw attention to yourselves."

Their faces lit up.

"Really?" Jelini asked.

"Really. You've earned a little fun. Just meet me back here in ten minutes. And remember—we're students visiting for the symposium. Nothing more."

They nodded eagerly and scattered into the crowd, leaving me to handle the more mundane details of our infiltration. I couldn't help but smile. I'd been holding the reins too tight.

I made my way to a quieter hallway branching off from the main celebration.

But before I could reach it, a new wave of partiers swept through, crowding the room even more thoroughly, led by two distinct groups in matching costumes. One bunch wore shimmering green outfits that made them look like floating pea pods, while the others were decked out in orange.

"Don't tell me you haven't placed bets between The Sweet Peas and the Orange Peels," someone nearby exclaimed, exasperated, seeing my confusion. "The wager is going to be massive tonight between our two biggest and baddest student clans as they wage brutal war against each other's wits to earn top scores in the identification trials."

The two groups faced off in the middle of the corridor, their leaders stepping forward with exaggerated formality.

"Your classification methodology is fundamentally flawed!" declared the Sweet Pea leader, triggering supportive cheers from their side.

"Your adherence to outdated categorical systems will be your downfall!" retorted the Orange Peel champion, earning equally enthusiastic backing.

I noticed Jim, Jelini, and Eggi had successfully made their exit toward the room with the gaming terminals.

Behind them, someone had programmed their environmental suit to project a constant stream of virtual sparks. Nothing actually flammable, just the visual representation of—in this case—a walking meteor.

The synthmead was clearly flowing freely—I could smell it in the air. The celebration had the feeling of something that had started formal and business-appropriate but was rapidly becoming less so, devolving toward the baser appetites of biological life everywhere.

I made my way through the crowds, trying to maintain my original purpose while taking in the scene. The vague, distant possibility occurred to me that perhaps the nanites were having an intoxicating effect on the ambient environment, but I quickly dropped my worry about such a silly concern. The costumes were far more interesting. I had never thought to apply engineering principles in such purely recreational ways.

In one corner, a student wearing a fully functional volcanic magma processing plant as a hat was earnestly explaining mineral classification theory to anyone who would listen. Nearby, someone had programmed the environmental controls to create localized zero-gravity pockets, and people were floating through them like bubbles in champagne.

I felt a presence beside me, someone who had been watching my progress through the crowd with some interest. I turned to find myself face to face with a man whose costume managed to be both elaborate and somehow understated—a technical masterpiece of fiber optics and reactive materials that suggested stellar phenomena without being gaudy about it. It reminded me of how it felt to extend my consciousness and try to count all the stars in my field of view.

"Not many people can sport a simulated junior techworker uniform so convincingly," he said, his voice carrying a hint of accent I couldn't quite place. "I'm Tooch Shawno."

There was something immediately disarming about him, a softness that contrasted with his height and build. He gave the impression of being slightly uncertain about how completely and totally attractive he was, as if he wasn't quite sure he deserved to be noticed.

"Mott Fortress," I replied, trying to maintain my focus on my mission.

"Fortress?" His eyes lit up with recognition. "You really are here from the IHC-111? What brings someone from maintenance all the way out to our humble School of Ore?" There was genuine curiosity in his tone, free of the condescension I usually encountered.

Maybe it was the general atmosphere of the party, or the lingering effects of our recent adventures, and maybe there really was something spiked in the ambient environment, but I found myself telling him everything—well, almost everything. About Beryl's call for help, about needing to borrow the Maltan's shuttle (I may have glossed over exactly how we'd "borrowed" it), about the merchant droids and the chase through the asteroid field.

Tooch listened with increasing amazement, occasionally asking surprisingly technical questions about ship systems and emergency protocols. He had seemed particularly interested in how I'd handled things escaping from Mudar's lair. Before I knew it, he was waving over a small group of his friends—other students wearing variations on the same stellar-themed costumes.

"You have to hear this," he told them, then launched into a retelling of our adventure, and it was only then that I realized all of what he described I had actually just experienced. Until that moment, it hadn't really settled in. Hearing his account of our flight from Mudar's facility sounded like a comedy of errors, like perhaps he believed I did such things all the time.

"So there they are," he was saying, gesturing expansively, "stuck in a royal-class shuttle with no ID codes, being chased by the most notorious salvage operation in the belt, when this absolute legend of a maintenance worker decides to rewire the entire routing system..."

Jim and Jelini emerged from the game room and made their way over to our table. Jelini was holding a glowing crystal trophy that pulsed with holographic patterns mimicking mineral formations. Where had they gotten such a trophy?

As Tooch finished regaling his friends with our story, his expression turned thoughtful. "You know," he said, reaching into one of his costume's many hidden pockets, "I always keep a spare synthpack for emergencies." He produced the glowing power unit, its value equivalent to several months of standard maintenance wages, and placed it in my palm, his hand divinely warm and comforting.

"I couldn't possibly—" I started, but he cut me off with a gentle smile.

"Consider it an investment in a promising junior member of our mining school." He turned to one of his friends, a shorter student whose deeply black costume gave every appearance of consisting of a material so dark it actively absorbed energy from its immediate surroundings. "Hey, Venn, you still carrying that backup unit?"

From a pocket somewhere in the darkness of Venn's garment, he produced three or four synthpacks with minimal hesitation, returning all but one to his pocket. He gave it to Tooch, who then turned it over to me, his fingers, brushing mine once more, warm and a little rough. "Just don't tell anyone in Advanced Resource Management. They're still mad about that incident with the decrystallization chamber."

"Your generosity... it's far too much, really. I can't possibly accept all this." I took a deep breath. "And I noticed that there was one part of my story you didn't say anything about. Beryl's ghost ship sighting. Do you know anything about that?"

"Ghost ship?" His eyebrows raised with interest as if teasing me. "You mean the phantom vessel that supposedly shadows the fleet?"

My heart raced. "So you've seen it too?"

"Oh, that old story," he chuckled, "It's been circulating around for generations. A mysterious vessel that appears and disappears, always just beyond sensor range."

Jelini's eyes widened. "That's exactly what Beryl was describing! She saw it just today."

Tooch's friend Venn, who had followed us, let out a hearty laugh. "Every mining outpost has their version of the ghost ship legend. Some say it's a failed prototype with experimental cloaking technology. Others think it's a hallucination caused by cosmic radiation affecting the visual cortex."

"But Beryl was so certain," I insisted, feeling a sinking disappointment. "It's what got us into this whole mess in the first place."

"Look," Tooch said, his voice softening, "your friend probably saw a sensor anomaly or light refraction through an asteroid mine's gas field."

"So this has all been for nothing?" Jim asked, his shoulders slumping.

"Not for nothing," I countered. "We uncovered evidence of a droid conspiracy. And we think the royals are backing them."

Tooch and Venn exchanged a glance.

"That's... complicated," Tooch said carefully. "The relationship between the royals and the autonomous droid collectives isn't what you might think."

"What do you mean?" I pressed.

"Let's just say there are good people on both sides of that particular divide," Venn interjected. "Some royals believe advancement requires embracing technological symbiosis. Others resist. Same with the droids. Some seek harmony with biological life, others don't."

"My advice?" Tooch added, "Stay out of it. The politics involved are ancient and tangled. Students like you have more immediate concerns."

I wanted to argue that we were already involved, whether we wanted to be or not, but I didn't have all the information. He believed that he was genuinely concerned for our safety.

"Just focus on getting your friend and heading home," he said. "Some mysteries are better left unexplored until you have more... resources at your disposal."

I was about to respond when a commotion erupted from the gaming room. Eggi came stumbling out, his face flushed, followed by an angry-looking young man wearing what had to be the most expensive costume in the room, all rare metals and precision engineering, and a dedicated antigrav generator creating a constant aura of floating accessories around him.

"How dare you!" the young man was shouting. "Do you have any idea—*any idea*—who I am?"

Behind him, a young woman in an equally elaborate outfit had her hands all over the antigrav man, trying to calm him down, while also shooting apologetic and pouting looks at Eggi. Judging from the lipstick on Eggi's mouth, face and neck, I could piece together through the chaos that this woman had perhaps made certain suggestions or advancements to Eggi, and her companion, who I now recognized as the Lieutenant Prince Aldrich from the royal fleet's junior diplomatic corps, was not a fan of her being so free and easy with her affection. Very much like one of the royal: antiquated, possessive, and protective.

"Time to go," Tooch said quickly, reading the situation. "I know the shop where that Rono brought your shuttle." He gestured toward a side exit. "Astero's Salvage is the best repair facility in this sector, if you know how to ask properly."

I looked at the synthpacks in my hand—not quite enough to cover Rono's demanded payment, but close.

"What about—" I gestured toward Eggi and the increasingly hostile prince.

"I'll handle it," Tooch assured me. "Aldrich owes me." He raised his voice. "Hey, Your Highness! Remember the zero-g metallurgy assignment with the iridium samples?"

The prince's face went from angry to concerned.

Eggi joined us as Tooch stepped between Aldrich and our group. "Your Highness, surely you remember how during the trials last semester, when Venna chose to partner with you instead of me for the final project? I could have made a scene, could have claimed some royal prerogative, but I respected her choice. Sometimes people make unexpected connections, Your Highness, and fighting about it only makes us look small, doesn't it? Perhaps we could extend the same courtesy to these visiting students... and maybe that's just Venna's way. You think?"

The prince made an ugly face of embarrassment before he nodded stiffly and turned away, his antigrav accessories wobbling slightly as he retreated.

"Follow me," Tooch said once he'd rejoined us. He led the way through a series of maintenance corridors I hadn't known existed. "Astero's isn't exactly on the official station maps, but trust me—it's exactly what you need right now."

As we walked, I couldn't help but notice how naturally he'd taken charge of the situation. He'd turned disaster into just another amusing party incident without missing a beat.

I clutched the synthpacks, feeling them against my palm. We were still far from solving all our problems, but if we could get the ship fixed, I felt like we might actually have a chance.

"So," Tooch asked as we walked, "want to hear about the time I accidentally inverted an entire asteroid's worth of gravity plates?"

Despite everything, I found myself smiling. Sometimes the best allies come from the most unexpected places.

As we walked, a memory surfaced unbidden of my first maintenance apprenticeship, working alongside Elder Fortress before she transferred to the BZT. We'd spent months restoring an ancient atmospheric processor, replacing corroded components and recalibrated delicate sensors. She never needed to tell me which tool to hand her —I just knew, like we shared the same mind. On her last day, we sat together in comfortable silence, watching the processor's status lights pulse with healthy green rhythms. Neither of us mentioned the transfer. Neither of us had to. She simply squeezed my shoulder and said, "You'll do fine, little bolt." It wasn't until after she'd gone that I realized how much I'd come to rely on someone I could have a wordless understanding with. Now, walking beside Tooch and the others, I felt how much I wanted to be part of something truly solid.

After leading us through a series of passages, we reached a maintenance airlock. He keyed in a sequence, waited as we passed through, then gave us a casual good-bye wave as the door shut, which left him on the other side. I realized he hadn't given me any way to contact him later, both to repay him and for other more emotional reasons I wasn't quite ready to examine.

THE MERCHANT OF MYSTERIES

Sometimes people trade in currencies we've forgotten how to recognize.

The airlock opened into an enormous space that stretched upward and outward into shadows. Ships in various states of repair hung suspended in maintenance cradles as automated systems and repair droids moved among them.

But what drew our attention was the booted figure slowly approaching us from a nearby workstation, his steps on the metal grating like a hammer pounding an anvil. Even at this distance I could tell he was on the shorter side. In fact, he would have barely reached my shoulder, were we to stand side by side, but his presence positively filled the space. If this was Fren Astero, he was no ordinary mechanic.

Every visible part of him that wasn't clearly original human tissue had been augmented or replaced with cybernetic components that seemed really old. I wondered why anyone would replace human tissue with old machinery? What kind of upgrade was that? Unless, the possibility emerged, these changes had been made a long time ago. That would make Astero older than anyone I'd met before. He certainly didn't look elderly.

He had a handlebar mustache that was robust, immense, and well-maintained. Gleaming metal and composite materials made up much of his visible body. One arm appeared to be a complete prosthetic, covered in tools that could extend and retract. His eyes—one organic, one a beastly dark optical array—studied us with the plutonic curiosity of deep space.

"Well," he said, his gruff voice more percussive than melodic, "what have we here?"

Jelini gasped. She clutched at Jim's arm, her eyes wide with awe.

"It's him," she whispered, but not quietly enough. "It's really him."

"Who?" Jim asked, though his tone suggested he already knew what was coming.

"Invisible Skylord Ultra," Jelini breathed. "He's taken physical form to help us in our time of need!"

The cyborg engineer, certainly Fren Astero, raised his organic eyebrow while his cybernetic eye whirred through several focus adjustments.

"Young lady," he began, but Jelini was already moving forward, her hands clasped in front of her.

Jelini raised the crystalline trophy she'd won from the video game high above her head, and its holographic patterns cast reflections across the vast dark room. She spoke with devotion.

"In the void between stars, you stand ever-present,
Through circuits and souls, your ever-presence holds true.
Invisible Ultra, bridge of all things,
Skylord where matter meets spirit, your wisdom holds true."
"From farthest space to smallest spark,
You light our way through ever-dark.
In every engine, every network,
Your sacred wisdom we yearn to see."

It was beyond embarrassing to hear her say such things out loud to a man we needed to ask a favor from.

But I thought I saw Astero's expression shift from annoyance to bemusement as she spoke.

"Young lady," he said again, and held out his hand in a gesture for her to stop, and he seemed at a loss for other words to say. His face became grim and he appraised the group of us. He once more became to all appearances a deeply cynical man, perhaps a very dangerous one, who we might possibly be making angry at this very moment. "What are you all trying to pull here?" Did he think we were taunting him?

Jelini lowered the trophy but her eyes remained bright with conviction. "The prophecies spoke of one who would bridge the physical and spiritual realms through mastery of machinery! Test us no more, I can see the truth in you."

Astero's organic eye crinkled with what I took to be a kind of sour amusement. "Since you are so good at seeing the truth, then you'll know I usually just go by Fren," he said carefully. He turned to address all of us. "Now, what brings a group of our young seeders to my humble establishment? Besides... deistic accusations."

I stepped forward, hoping to steer the conversation back to practical matters before Jelini could elaborate further. "We need repairs on a royal-class shuttle. It was dropped off by a droid named Rono."

Both of Astero's eyes—organic and mechanical—focused on me. "You know this Rono well?"

"Not exactly," I admitted. "It's complicated." I shifted my legs. "It seems like a nice droid."

"'Nice droid?'" Astero glowered disgustedly at us, each in turn. "You must be royal after all. Rono's not a 'nice droid.' It's the very best. You should count yourselves lucky."

He gestured for us to follow him deeper into the workshop. As we walked, Jelini clutched the trophy tightly before her and continued to stare at him with undisguised wonder.

The workshop stretched away into cool darkness like some ancient temple to mechanical sacrifice. Oily chains hung from the ceiling, swaying slightly in currents from the ventilation system, their links catching the dim light. Hydraulic fluid and coolant had left luminescent streaks down the walls, with flecks of ore and rust like gore in a shadowy meat locker.

Iron tables lined the space, their surfaces crowded with dismembered machine parts and chunks of semiorganic ore awaiting repurification. Some components still leaked fluids that collected in wide green and deep plasma-blue pools on the floor. The air was thick with the sharp tang of heated metal, with the musty smell of aged lubricants and mineral dust.

Astero's metal feet rang against the deck plates with metronomic precision as he led us deeper into his domain. Occasionally, something would move in the darkness beyond the lights—perhaps automated systems, or maybe something else entirely.

We walked beneath massive hoists and cranes overhead that disappeared into the gloom, their cables ascending up into darkness like spider silk. The stripped-down skeletal frames of what might have once been ships hung from some of them.

The cold seeped up through the floor, and it made the metal railings and work surfaces uncomfortably frigid to touch. This was a place where machines came to be dissected, their components sorted and categorized.

"The prophecies said you would create a place where all forms of life could be healed," Jelini commented, watching a small repair drone slowly make rapid, violent adjustments to a disembodied machine heart.

"The prophecies seem remarkably well-informed about my business model," Astero replied dryly. I wondered why he didn't deny her accusations outright.

We reached what appeared to be Astero's main workshop, a circular chamber dominated by a holographic design table that projected schematics of various vessels in glowing detail. The Maltan's shuttle was there among them, rotating slowly on a zero-G levihoist as diagnostic data scrolled on several nearby hoverscreens in cool semitransparent blue.

"About payment," I began, nervously producing the synthpacks Tooch and his friend had given us. "We have... these, and—"

Astero's cybernetic eye flashed red. "Insufficient," he stated flatly. "The materials alone for the diameter-B realignment cost more than that. Not to mention the droid-minutes it took to restore the many proprietary calibration sequences required for... *royal*-class vessels." He shook his head. "The ship stays here until proper payment is arranged."

"But we need it," Jelini stepped forward, her voice conveying her embarrassingly absolute fervor. "Just as you needed the Original Armor when you first manifested in the physical realm."

My mouth dropped open. My palm came to my forehead.

Astero's organic eye narrowed while his mechanical one cycled through several scanning patterns.

"The Original Armor," he repeated slowly. "You know of this?"

Jelini's hands moved to the crystalline trophy. In this room of cold shadows and brute disassembly, it was captivating the way the light moved through it, the patterns that shift and changed... perhaps it wasn't a simple token. Perhaps it was worth something.

"The texts speak of how ISU first appeared to the ancient engineers," she said, kneeling before him with the trophy. "Wearing armor made of pure light, each ringlet containing a different facet of truth." She held out the crystal construct. "This is not worthy remuneration, of course, but its endless variability reminds of the Original Armor."

Astero took the trophy with his bearlike human hand, his various scanning systems appraising it with curiosity. "Most believe the Original Armor was lost in the Founding Wars," He trailed off, seemingly lost in thought.

"There were proverbs that came from those battles," he said suddenly, his voice distant. "'In the reflection of true light, all paths become clear and one.'" He gave a short laugh. "But then, there was also: 'The false path is the one most obscured by certainty.'"

The holographic displays continued with their streams of cool blue diagnostic details, flickering in the dark warehouse. Astero stood perfectly still, both eyes fixed on something none of us could see.

"You know," he said finally, "I had forgotten something rather important about Freyan cruisers." His organic eye twinkled with what might have been mischief.

He placed the crystalline trophy carefully on his workbench, then made a gesture that caused the Maltan shuttle's main airlock to hiss open.

"Your ship awaits you," he announced. "And as for payment..." he glanced at the headpiece, "Leave the synthpacks with me and let's say we've reached an understanding."

"Really?" I couldn't believe it.

"Go," he said, already turning back to his work.

We stood, frozen and unsure whether he meant earnestly that, after all this, he wanted us to leave, and that, despite all odds, we could actually do so in our own ship.

"Go!" he said again, this time with a furious brief laugh. "Before I remember a different truth."

I wouldn't forgive myself if I needed to be told a third time. As we hurried onboard the deck of our newly-repaired shuttle, I heard Astero's laughter following us, interspersed with what sounded like a deep, sonorous voice humming an unfamiliar tune.

Aside from the unmistakable odor of fresh steelpaste, the shuttle looked in all ways better than new, its hull gleaming with fresh molecular bonding, every system optimized beyond factory specifications.

Jelini held up a hand. "Wait," she said. "I should have done this the first time."

"Jelini, don't—" I started, but she was already halfway out the airlock.

I raced after her, mortified by this further delay when we'd just been granted our freedom.

She ran to the front of the ship, rummaging through the pockets of her uniform until she produced a many-colored ribbon. With ceremonial care, she hung it like a garland over the ship's foremost antenna.

"There," she said, carefully adjusting the placement of the garland. "It's a charm that lets all the migrant spirits of space, the souls and fragments passing by, know that this vessel is special."

She smiled at me.

Astero raised one eyebrow. He hadn't otherwise moved.

I patted Jelini on the shoulder and we raced back onto the ship. The door sealed behind us with a satisfying hiss of finality.

"Did that all really just happen?" Jim asked.

"Skylord works in mysterious ways," Jelini replied with complete seriousness and for all appearance, a rapt heart.

I had pretty much hit my limit for how much eccentricity from Jelini I could tolerate for the time being, but right now, we had a working ship and a clear path to Beryl. Sometimes, I was learning, it's better not to question the strange gifts the universe occasionally provides. It could be far better to let people have space to be themselves and not worry so much about what conditioning decreed was proper.

We slid the ship through the series of pneumatic buffers that cycled us through three separate airlocks, each one opening just as the previous sealed, a smooth transition from the warehouse's pressurized environment to open space. The sequence felt impossibly well-engineered, like we were being guided by an invisible hand. As the final lock opened, revealing the star-filled void, I caught that last glimpse of Astero through a small porthole into his facility, and I could have sworn I saw him in the docking bay below, still examining the crystalline headpiece, his mechanical components catching the light in ways that, just for a moment, did make him look like something more than merely human.

THE GRACE OF SECOND CHANCES

Bx5's serene emanations offer anything but peace.

The Maltan's shuttle handled like a dream after Astero's improvements. You couldn't tell to look at it—it looked exactly the same as it did when we'd first set foot in it before the misadventure in the asteroids, except that it was perhaps cleaner. But everything about it felt better. Whatever he and his crew had done to the propulsion systems made the controls respond to the lightest touch, and the navigation interface seemed to anticipate my intentions exactly as I formed them. For the first time since this adventure began, I felt truly confident about our chances.

We were taking a wide approach vector toward the PNO, staying just near enough to the approved traffic lanes to avoid drawing attention or finding ourselves in another renegade droid debacle. Through the viewport, the massive bulk of Processing Station Alpha-1 stretched away to our right, its myriad lights reminding me of ancient cities I'd seen in historical archives. We passed by other ships and maintenance vehicles and the occasional cloud of dust and a few asteroids.

Our vector had brought our ship near to Bx5-1a2-Micro, so I adjusted our course ever so slightly to give us all a chance to bask in the beautiful subvisible color fields surrounding it. Within moments, the asteroid's famous energy emanations were tangible, and we found ourselves awash in sheets of subtle nonphysical colors that rippled through space.

The asteroid hung against the starfield exactly where it had been this morning when Tam had canceled our romantic getaway, and at the time, I had believed him when he said he needed to debug his compartment AI. But there, unmistakable in its custom configuration of gleaming hull plates and massive engine array, was his personal racer. Just where it would be parked if we were having the romantic picnic we'd planned. And it wasn't alone—it was docked alongside a sleek vessel I couldn't place the origins of.

And not too far away from the two rafts was a transparent dome exactly like what would be used if we were having the picnic we'd planned. But if Tam wasn't in there with me...

My stomach lurched as I realized what this might mean. At this distance, the dome was little more than a dot, and there was considerable glare on it, so I adjusted the viewport to bring up the magnifier.

I recognized Tam's silhouette. Next to him was another figure. The two of them were sitting very close.

"Mott?" Jim's voice seemed to come from very far away. "Are you okay? Your hands are..."

I looked down to see my knuckles white on the control yoke.

Jelini leaned forward from her station, following my gaze. "Is that... someone else's vessel?"

"Computer! Magnify," I ordered, and the shuttle's enhanced systems immediately brought the scene into sharper focus.

Tam sat on a picnic blanket under a protective atmospheric dome with a woman I recognized as Jain, one of the rising stars of the royal diplomatic corps. She moved with the grace of someone who had received extensive microgravity training, and her skin-tight uniform left little to be imagined about her desirability when it came to physique. Jain was beautiful. She was also known to be a "wardrober," someone so sexually promiscuous that they had a new partner every time you looked at them, so it could be said that these people were known for treating romantic relationships as casually as changing clothes.

I watched through the viewport as Tam leaned in close to Jain, his arm draped casually around her shoulders. The way they sat together spoke of easy intimacy—none of the nervous energy or careful distance that had always characterized our interactions. He was laughing at something she'd said, his head thrown back in mirth. I was trying to recall if I'd ever made him laugh like that.

The artificial atmosphere dome created a slight distortion, like looking through old glass, but the display's magnification made it possible to make out the details—how his fingers played with a strand of her hair, how she pressed against him. They shared a bottle of what was probably real wine, not synthmead. The kind of luxury only royals could afford.

The picnic I'd planned seemed childish now—my carefully packed meal of standard rations suddenly felt embarrassingly inadequate compared to the spread laid out before them. He'd always told me that he never cared about such things, that it was my company he valued. He was always so interested to hear me talk about my day, about the work I had done.

"He *lied* to me," I said, my voice sounding strange in my own ears. "This morning, he canceled our plans. He'd seemed so sincere, he gave me this whole excuse, I'd actually felt sorry for him, but he's out here. With her."

My throat felt tight. "He wasn't debugging anything," I said quietly. "He was planning this. With her."

For a moment, I disassociated. I just stared blankly at how the Maltan shuttle's polished surface caught the starlight from the viewport, and reflected it across the cabin in patterns that danced over the control consoles.

My hands trembled on the navigation interface from the storm brewing inside me. The image of Tam and Jain together burned in my mind. My throat constricted as I tried to swallow past the knot of betrayal lodged there. All those evenings I'd spent talking through ins and outs of maintenance to him, believing he was genuinely interested in my work...

"We're making a pit stop," I announced, already adjusting our course. The shuttle banked steeply toward the asteroid.

The rational part of my mind knew it was a bad idea, that we were already dealing with enough complications. But something deeper had taken hold—a vengeful need to understand exactly what was happening.

"Approaching docking range," Jim reported unnecessarily. "Do you want me to—"

"No," I cut him off, more sharply than intended. "I'll handle this."

The shuttle's enhanced systems made it easy to establish a parking orbit without being immediately obvious to the other vessels.

"Oh, Mott," Jelini said softly. "I'm so sorry."

The ship docked nimbly at one of the asteroid's auxiliary maintenance airlocks, the same one Tam and I had used a few times before for our own meetings. My fingers moved automatically through the familiar unlock sequence. The codes hadn't changed.

The access tunnel was exactly as I remembered it—a narrow passage carved through the rock, reinforced with structural bracing and lined with basic life support systems. Emergency lights cast everything in a dim blue glow. The air held that mineral smell unique to Bx5-1a2-Micro cut by the brisk odor of active force fields.

"Maybe we should wait—" Eggi started to suggest, but fell silent at my expression.

We moved quietly through the passage, but our footsteps echoed despite our best efforts. As I unscrewed the dome's light entrance hatch, I could hear their voices: Tam's familiar laugh, and another, flagrantly musical one that had to be Jain's.

The dome's internal atmospheric systems masked the sound of our arrival. I could see them clearly with my naked eyes now—Tam lounging on expensive cushions, Jain practically in his lap, both of them completely oblivious to our presence.

I let the hatch slam shut behind us. The sound of laughter stopped as they turned to face us. Tam's expression shifted from relaxed happiness to shock to something else—it didn't resemble guilt as much as annoyance at being interrupted.

"Mott!" he managed, scrambling to his feet. "It's so good to see you. What are you doing here?"

"I have to say, your debugging technique is a bit unorthodox." I eyed Jain. "Although, that is a real mess of code you're working on."

Before either could react, I strode forward and stomped right in the middle of their elaborate picnic setup, and with a kick sent exotic delicacies and wine spattering.

"Mott, stop!" Tam shouted, but Eggi took the cue and was already in motion as well, knocking over their expensive portable entertainment system. In the scuffle, he managed to snatch a high-end datapad from Tam's bag, while "accidentally" crushing another one under his boot.

"Oops," Eggi said. He pocketed the intact pad while pretending to help clean up the mess. "These things are so fragile."

Jain rose to her feet, "Do you have any idea who you're dealing with? The fleet won't take kindly to this."

"To what?" I shot back. "To finding out your perfect little world isn't as exclusive as you thought?"

"You absolute child," Jain spat, brushing at her stained uniform. "This is exactly why we need to elevate beyond your kind of... working-class thinking."

"At least I know who I am," I shot back. "At least I'm not a royal bootlicker."

Jelini hung back, clearly uncomfortable with the situation but full of wide grins at the drama. The tension in the dome was palpable, made more dizzying by the way the energy emanations from the asteroid cast everything in shifting, otherworldly colors.

Tam's face darkened. "Always so patriotic, aren't you, Mott? Did you ever think maybe there's more to life than being a good little seeder?" He laughed coldly. "I could never decide if you were too easy to manipulate or just too boring to bother with."

Jim's fist connected with Tam's jaw before I even registered him moving. The second punch caught Tam's eye as he staggered backward, and it sent him sprawling into the remains of their ruined picnic.

I grabbed Jim's sleeve, pulling him back toward the airlock. "We're done here."

As we retreated, I caught one last glimpse of Tam sprawled among the scattered food and broken technology, holding his face and looking utterly confused about how his perfect day had gone so wrong.

The shuttle's airlock closed behind us with a satisfying thunk.

As we settled back into the main cabin, I made sure everyone was securely strapped in. I focused on the practical details to keep my mind off what had just happened.

"Is everyone okay?" I asked, my voice still shaking slightly.

Jim flexed his hand, knuckles already slightly swollen. "Never better," he said with a fierce grin. "Actually feeling stronger than ever."

"That was brave of you," Jelini told him softly. "Standing up for Mott like that."

I noticed Eggi shifting in his seat, pulling something from his pocket—the royal datapad he'd managed to snatch during the chaos. His eyes widened as he studied its screen.

"You stole that?"

"Borrowed," he corrected. His face looked grim. "Um, guys?" he said. "I think you need to see this."

The datapad displayed technical documentation, detailed schematics of the IHC's propulsion systems. But more than that, there were notes, calculations, and logs.

"Tam was spying," I realized, the betrayal cutting even deeper. "Using me to get information about our technology."

"Not just the technology," Eggi said grimly, scrolling through more files. "Check out these outbound records. He's been reporting stuff to the royal fleet for months."

"Look at this." His fingers traced details across the fractured screen. "Some kind of research. About the capacities of the engine cores."

The screen flickered to life to reveal schematics that made my blood run cold. They were detailed diagrams of the engine's core components—classified information that only senior maintenance workers should have access to. These details should never leave an airgapped machine. If they fell into the wrong hands...

"These are my access codes," I whispered. "He must have copied them while watching me work." The realization kept hitting me like punches to my chest. "All those times he asked about my job, showed interest in the engine maintenance, he was gathering intelligence for some cadre of royals."

The screen flickered, and I saw messages between Tam and several royal fleet officials. The conversations discussed a deviation in mission parameters—abandoning the seeding of diverse biological life in favor of what it called the ReGenesis program, which would alter the evolution of any worlds they reached.

"They're planning to change our mission without telling the other ships," I whispered, scanning the text. "These messages show they've been developing something in secret, and planning to implement it without consensus from all three ships."

Jim stepped forward. "'Trust, once broken, cannot be repaired through mere regret. The truth stands independent of our wishes.'"

Whatever he was quoting, it was meant to be supportive, I knew, but somehow his philosophical distance just made everything feel worse.

This wasn't just about the royals having access to schematics or privileged information—everyone had been young on the IHC at some point; all sorts of information flowed readily between ships. This was about a covert decision to alter humanity's legacy in the cosmos, made by a secret group who believed they knew better than everyone else.

"The seeders have always operated by consensus," Jim said, his face pale. "Every major decision about our mission is supposed to be approved by all three ships."

"Not anymore, apparently," I replied, the weight of the betrayal sinking in. As much as Tam had hurt me, what he and the others were working toward might threaten the foundation of our society.

"That lying, manipulative..." I trailed off, too angry to continue.

"Mott," Jelini said softly, and placed her hand on my arm. "We need to focus. Beryl's waiting."

"Mott," Eggi started, "what are you—"

My fingers had moved toward the weapons controls almost of their own accord.

"Mott," Jelini's voice came softly from behind me, and her eyes were wide with panic. "This isn't you."

But wasn't it? Wasn't this exactly who I was—someone who fixed things, who made broken systems work again? And wasn't this just another kind of repair?

The targeting system blinked to life beneath my fingertips. Its interface bathed my hands in cool blue light as it calculated firing solutions. The Freyan-class shuttle, posh and utilitarian, had only a minimal weapons system, as our previous experience with the renegades had proven. But all I needed was one clean shot. That's all it would take to show Tam how I felt about him using me.

And why not? Hadn't his actions proven that he was deeply treasonous? The ReGenesis program sounded all too compatible with the overthrow plans of the renegade droids. Such a scheme would undermine the whole mission. What of all the generations that had sacrificed their lives to seed life across the cosmos? Now a handful of elites were deciding to replace that with their own vision—hybrid organisms programmed to evolve along predetermined paths.

My mind flashed forward through millennia—planets that instead of flourishing with the wild beauty of natural evolution would be seeded with ordered, mechanized, efficient life. Lifeforms designed from the ground up to be easily dominated. Worlds where nothing truly free would ever be allowed to exist. Billions of potential beings who would never know what it meant to choose their own destiny because their very DNA had been programmed to merge with machines.

All decided by people like Tam and Jain. People who believed they knew better than everyone else.

"Maybe the merchant droids were right," I whispered, the words bitter on my tongue. "About the age of biological dominance ending. At least machines are honest about their programming."

I considered again my finger on the trigger. "He deserves it," I whispered, not sure if I was trying to convince Jelini or myself.

"Maybe," she replied. "But you don't deserve to become the kind of person who would do this."

"Mott..." Jim started, but I continued, the darkness inside me finding its voice.

"No, really, look at us—generations of seeders, thinking we're spreading life across the galaxy. But what kind of life? Even if we succeed, what kind of life are we? The kind that betrays, that lies, that uses love as a tool for espionage?" The targeting system offered multiple vectors now, each one showing a high probability of success. "Maybe we deserve to be replaced. Maybe the droids would do a better job."

"That's not true," Jelini protested, but there was a tremor in her voice.

I could feel the others drawing away from me—not physically, but emotionally.

"So what's your solution?" Eggi asked. "Give up everything that makes us human because feeling things hurts too much?"

The targeting computer waited. It would execute whatever command I gave it with perfect efficiency—and that suddenly seemed like the most terrifying thing in the universe.

That's what Tam had done—executed his mission regardless of the emotional damage it would cause. He had made himself into a kind of machine of ambition, and the result was something far worse than being pulled around by human emotions. Just because he didn't feel empathy didn't mean he wasn't still governed by his cravings.

The weapons system powered down with a soft sigh as I released the controls. The darkness inside me didn't go away.

Nobody spoke as I turned the shuttle away from the asteroid. But I could feel the rift my words had created, and I wasn't in a position yet to be able to mend things.

I looked out at the stars—the ones I used to count with Tam, trying to see as many as I could hold in my vision at once. But right now I didn't feel like trying to see every star at once. I would choose the ones I focused on, and they would be the ones that mattered enough to navigate by.

The shuttle's enhanced systems handled perfectly as we cut our approach path toward the medical sector of the PNO-80. Asteroid bits and scattered debris drifted past.

"Standard approach vector," I reported mechanically, my voice hollow even to my own ears. "We should reach medical docking in approximately twelve minutes."

The events at the asteroid played through my mind in a sickening loop—Tam with Jain, the datapad with all those access codes, the casual way he'd spoken about using me. I tried to focus on our mission instead. Simple, really: dock at the medical sector, find Beryl, get her out, return to the IHC-111, and hide every trace of our unauthorized adventure from the Elder Maltans.

Jim monitored the secondary systems and occasionally glanced my way with poorly disguised concern. Eggi remained uncharacteristically silent. The empty space where Jelini should have been felt like an accusation. I thought for a moment where she might have stormed off to, then I looked down and saw her life sign reading registering from the airlock. I double-checked that none of the systems in there could accidentally be opened, and chose to give her the space she needed to sulk and process all that had just happened.

I ran a hand through my hair, my fingers catching on tangles. The control room felt too small, too close. "Look," I said to Eggi and Jim, my voice raw, "I'm sorry about what happened back there. That was... I don't even know how to make it right." My hands trembled as I remembered the targeting system humming beneath my fingertips, how close I'd come. "I was exhausted, but that's no excuse. I should never have put any of you in this situation."

Jim leaned forward, his eyes serious. "But Mott, we wanted to come."

"Yeah," Eggi nodded. "I think you're overlooking the fact that we've turned out to be pretty competent in these types of situations." He cast a sidelong glance at Jim. "We get into trouble all the time."

Jim elbowed him. "Well, more like *he* gets into trouble."

Something about the way they could still joke after everything we'd seen, and what I'd almost done—broke something loose inside me. A laugh escaped my throat, surprising even me, and that's when I felt the wetness on my cheeks.

I wiped at my face, embarrassed. "I can't believe what I actually considered doing back there."

Eggi's expression darkened. "Honestly, it's not out of the question." His voice dropped. "That kind of intent—to destroy another person out of rage—it's not good. Or what Jelini would call good anyway." His eyes widened suddenly. "But Mott, once we hand all this data over—and it's very incriminating data—to the judicial team, they'll see how treasonous it all is." He swallowed. "I don't use that word lightly, Mott. Treason."

The word hung in the air between us. My gaze drifted to the sealed compartment where Jelini had disappeared. "Jelini," I called, "will you come in here?"

"I'm working on something top secret, Mott!" Her muffled voice carried through the sealed door.

Jim smiled. "We can leave her. It's fine." He met my eyes. "She needs space too, after everything. And I think all that data gave her some sort of idea."

I nodded, trusting that he understood his sister, and turned back to the viewport.

The bulk of the PNO-80 grew larger in our viewport, its hull far less worse for wear than the other two ships of our fleet. Its surface was dotted with countless many-colored lights that formed scale-like patterns against the metal. Beryl was in there somewhere, waiting for us. I wondered if she'd discovered something worth all this trouble, or if her paranoia had finally led her down one too many rabbit holes.

"Initiating docking procedures," I said. "Let's hope the Maltans don't decide to check their ship's logs anytime soon."

WHEN THE YOUNG LEAD

She'd mapped the impossible and disappeared into the space between what we knew and what we feared. Of course she had.

After coming to stasis in the docking bay, I noticed Jelini's life sign reading depart from the shuttle the instant the airlock doors opened. She'd slipped away without a word.

"She's run away!"

"She won't wander far," Jim said. "Jelini's impulsive, but she's not reckless. She knows you really care about her."

"We can't let her just wander off," I said, already jogging toward the airlock and waving the others to come with me.

Eggi nodded. "Three pairs of eyes are better than one for finding both Beryl and Jelini. We stick together from here on. Us two," he put his arm over Jim's shoulder, "and Captain Mott."

I wanted to correct him on the technicalities of rank, but grinned instead.

"Alright," I said, squaring my shoulders and heading out into the docking bay. "Let's move."

Perhaps now I understood why Beryl's discovery had seemed so urgent. Whatever game Tam and Jain were playing, it was clearly part of something much bigger—something worth fighting for, despite my broken heart.

In a corner alcove of the docking bay, I found Jelini's discarded storage locker key, and with it a hastily scrawled note on the back of a maintenance requisition form: "Going to fix what's broken. I solved the clue of the constellation cluster." The handwriting was unmistakably Jelini's—loopy and ornate, with those annoying spiraled dots she always put over her i's.

"What does she mean, she solved the clue?" Jim scrunched his face at the note. "What clue? And what's broken?"

Eggi snatched the note and examined it. "Look. See these dots?" He held the page at an angle so docking bay lights revealed an array of white dots across its surface. "These patterns... I wonder if they match the coordinates we found on the back of the datapad in Mudar's office?"

Jim brought out the stolen datapad and turned it over. When compared with Jelini's note, the pattern was more or less a match. On Jelini's drawing, there were additional markings—a spot with a square around it, recognizable as the bay we had entered, with dots between it and another prominent dot labeled "central hub," as if measuring the distance or doing some sort of triangulation.

"See?" Eggi traced the pattern with his fingertip. "These marks. She's mapped out a route."

I compared the scans I had of the immediate surroundings, and what he was saying checked out. However she had managed to produce such a map, she had also done it impressively fast.

"That means Jelini is headed to this dot at the end," I said, pointing to the final point in the sequence.

Jim tapped the faint inscription we'd found in Mudar's office. A single word scratched beside an identical dot at the end of Jelini's pattern: "FLUX."

Whatever Flux was, it was important enough for Mudar to take note—and apparently Jelini believed it was worth risking everything to reach it.

"No time to waste," I said. "Let's go."

AMONG THE AUGMENTED

In a ward full of people surrendering their bodies to machinery, Beryl clutched her removable scanner and remembered: the ability to choose otherwise is the last freedom they can't augment away.

From several of the staff in the observation room, Beryl caught fragments of conversation she wished she hadn't heard: "...unstable signature..." "...temporal displacement..." "...need to contain the spread..."

The entrance of the man with radiation burns had caused a commotion that had drawn more staff into the room. She'd edged closer in an attempt to uncover another piece of evidence for her theories. For years, she'd collected fragments of possible truths, each one reinforcing her suspicion that the royal fleet concealed technologies beyond what they shared with the IHC.

But they'd whisked the patient away too quickly, and it left her feeling frustrated, just another person among the agitated observers. Whatever that man had encountered might be the key to everything—the missing piece that would validate all her years of watchfulness.

She thought she could make out some sort of a preacher or impassioned public speaker standing nearby, or maybe just someone who had taken too much (or not enough) of a certain kind of medicine. It was a man delivering an impromptu sermon about symbiosis, how the relationship between organic and mechanical life was sacred, predestined. "As all the great clan leaders equally foresaw since before our time began," he intoned, "the merging of flesh and circuit brings us closer to perfection."

Beryl fought the urge to laugh. If only they knew what the early seeders had really written about the dangers of dependency on machine intelligence. Or—had they said that?

She needed to find her scanner. More importantly, she needed to find a way to get her evidence about the ghost ship to someone she knew she could trust. But first, she had to survive long enough to make that happen.

Based on her prior research, she believed that it was possible that the ward's monitoring systems were everywhere, disguised as decorative fixtures. The royals didn't need obvious security, because real power lay in making people police themselves.

If only Mott would arrive. She was alone with her unverifiable suspicions in a room full of people who might be dangerous, delusional, or—most terrifying of all—perfectly normal.

"Symbiosis, my friends, and my enemies too," the preacher droned on. "Symbiosis is the way forward..."

Beryl nonchalantly paced toward what she believed was a hallway, trying to look like she belonged here while plotting her next move. Somewhere in this labyrinth of well-decorated rooms and false civility, there had to be a way of finding answers. Or at least getting ahold of someone who could give her some working digital contacts.

Beryl might have slunk away entirely, but she overheard something in a couple's conversation that made her pause—something about "compatibility protocols."

As it turned out, it wasn't just a couple. A small crowd was gathering near what was probably the ward's central atrium, drawn by the sound of passionate speech. A figure stood on a makeshift platform—tall, rail-thin, wearing the elaborate robes of what Beryl recognized as a Sympathetic, one of the new quasi-religious movements that had sprung up in the fleet. With disappointment, she realized it was the same preacher she had been hearing earlier. She had walked in a circle.

"The age of separation is ending!" the preacher proclaimed. "We must embrace the symbiosis! Human and machine, flesh and circuit, all becoming one perfect system!"

The crowd murmured appreciatively. Many of them bore easily visible cybernetic enhancements—augmented eyes, enhanced limbs, data ports in temples and wrists. They were walking the walk, she supposed, committed to a path she couldn't imagine choosing for herself.

Cybernetic enhancement remained controversial throughout the fleet, and for good reason. It was a one-way journey in most cases. Replace an eye or a hand, stuff a few modules into your limbs, and there was rarely a way back.

Some argued these alterations made you less human. Others that they made you more human, since technology was the ultimate expression of a purely human creative power.

For Beryl, watching these altered people nod along to the preacher's sermon, the issue was simpler. She wanted the best technology, but more than that, she wanted choice. She wanted her scanner and contacts because she could remove them, could shut them off, could step away when she chose. She craved information but feared dependence. What happened when the systems failed? When the collective that maintained them changed direction?

Her proximal scanner let her see beyond normal human perception without sacrificing her autonomy. These people had made a different choice. They had surrendered that final barrier between themselves and their technology, trusting not just their apparatus, but the worldviews of those who programmed them.

Things happened to gear just as they happened to biological systems, whether by getting compromised in one way or another or else breaking down. And when that hardware was wired directly into your brain, what recourse did you have?

"The old ways of the Seeders, brave as they were, must give way to evolution!" the preacher continued. "Why spread life across the galaxy when we can transcend life itself? Why remain bound by flesh when we can achieve true symbiosis?"

Beryl pressed closer, trying to appear part of the crowd while studying their reactions. It was strange to think that all of them more or less belonged to the same collective, and yet how different everyone was fighting to be. Those aboard the IHC, BZT, and PNO carried on lives and missions with such adamant separative consciousness, it was maddening to track. How could this be true while at the same time their mission was to seed humanity?

Perhaps these people had been put here as a ploy to create a scene or distract people so no one would notice the arrival of the mysterious vessel. Or was the ship's arrival somehow stimulating this fervor in people? Had it brought some mysterious influence upon them? The connections seemed plausible, even likely, yet she couldn't prove any of it yet.

Beryl knew she was at a disadvantage. She didn't get away from the IHC often enough to know if this was normal behavior for the PNO inhabitants. Older people were strange at the best of times, especially these with their cybernetic modifications and cryptic references to protocols from previous generations.

What was happening back on the IHC? Had anyone there spotted it? If the mysterious ship represented what she suspected—a confrontation with a separate human vessel on a separate ancient mission—the implications may shatter the foundation of their entire society. It would mean thousands of lives across generations had been spent on a mission that might come to nothing in her lifetime.

She just hoped Mott would get her message in time. What was taking her so long?

THE MAP IN THE MESSAGE

Jelini assaults a communications buoy to either expose a ghost ship or prove paranoia is contagious.

Following Jelini's trail took us into rougher areas of the PNO—areas I couldn't have known existed, because officially they didn't exist yet. These were new sections under active construction—skeletal corridors with exposed frameworks, half-finished rooms with temporary lighting strung across open ceilings, and unfinished passageways where construction equipment lay abandoned between shifts.

The royal fleet was expanding the PNO at a significant scale. Tool crates and hardware containers were stacked in makeshift pyramids against partially installed bulkheads. Bundles of fiber optic cabling hung from ceiling fixtures, their ends splayed open and awaiting connection.

Everywhere the smell of welding compounds and fresh sealant.

"Why build so much, so fast?" Jim whispered, running his fingers along a freshly fabricated support beam.

The further we ventured into this incomplete labyrinth, the more obvious it became that whatever the royal fleet was constructing, it wasn't designed according to standard seeder specifications. The proportions felt wrong—doorways slightly lower, corridors wider, control interfaces positioned at heights that would be awkward for average human use.

We rounded another corner, and a shape moving in the distance caught my attention. Through a viewport looking out into space, I could see a small figure in a battered maintenance suit attempting to maneuver along the ship's exterior.

"What in Smith's name is she doing—" Jim pointed out the viewport. "Out there?" He looked over at me, terrified.

Through the viewport, we watched Jelini in a weathered space suit blasting her way into the distance toward a massive communications buoy. The base of the buoy was around the size of the Maltan ship. Onto this base stood a long cylinder with a bulbous pentagonal base and blinking lights on its far end.

"And where the hell are we going to get suits?" Eggi was already looking around wildly. I appreciated his immediate assumption that we were going to pursue her out there.

Actually, there was no shortage of equipment scattered around the area. In very little time I'd managed to spot a storage rack with emergency EVA gear. "There!"

We scrambled into the suits as quickly as possible and found our way to a small airlock. Inside, the pressure equalized and warning lights slowly cycled from red to yellow. When the outer door finally slid open and the void greeted us, we were ready.

Stepping out onto the hull of the PNO was disorienting. This wasn't the smooth, completed exterior I'd seen in training videos—this was raw construction, skeletal and exposed. Half-installed hull plates created a patchwork landscape of metal and shadow. Support struts jutted out like the ribs of some massive beast, and bundles of cabling hung suspended in the vacuum, their ends not yet connected to anything, many of them blinking intermittently.

The stars surrounding us were bright, and the curvature of the massive ship stretched away beneath our boots. Our magnetic soles clicked against the metal as we navigated this strange borderland between finished vessel and open space.

We climbed up a partially installed communications array, using the latticework of support beams as an improvised ladder. From this higher vantage point, we could see Jelini more clearly, her small form silhouetted against the emptiness.

"We could try jumping," Jim suggested, his voice tinny through the suit's comm system. "Use the thrust from our propulsion packs to reach her."

I considered the small maneuvering units built into our suits. These weren't designed for long-distance travel—just enough thrust to navigate around a ship during repairs, maybe reposition yourself if you drifted away from your work site. The distance to Jelini looked deceptively close, but in vacuum, miscalculating even slightly would send us tumbling into the void.

"Too risky," I decided. "And we'd be completely exposed. Security would spot us out here immediately. I'm surprised they're not already after her."

"What about the comms?" Eggi suggested, already examining the control panel on his forearm. "Unless she deactivated her system, we should be able to find her on a channel."

We activated our suit communication arrays and cycled through the available frequencies. The maintenance bands were crowded with chatter, but nothing from Jelini. I tried the emergency channel—still nothing.

"Wait," Jim said suddenly. "Try modulating to frequency 117.3. That's what they use for covert operations in 'Wraiths Among Us'."

"That's a game," I reminded him, but tried it anyway.

A burst of static, then: "—repeating, don't come closer! I've almost—" Jelini's voice, breathless but determined.

Beyond her, I spotted a figure in a black environment suit had approached her. The figure was attempting to pull her away from the buoy, where she clung to an access panel, her fingers still typing commands into the interface. With surprising strength, she kicked out, and it sent her attacker tumbling backward through the vacuum.

"Jelini!" I called into the comm. "We're coming to help!"

"No! Stay back!" Her voice was urgent. "I need to finish this."

"What are you even trying to do?" I demanded.

"This isn't a regular communications buoy," Jelini's voice came back, breathless as she continued typing. "It's a dampening field generator designed to mask the signature of the ghost ship's flux drive!"

"Flux drives don't exist," I said.

"You'll see!" Jelini replied. "The royals, Mudar, Crasp—they're all in on it. This system is designed to hide the ship Beryl saw. If I can disable it, everyone in the fleet will be able to see the ghost ship's movements!"

The figure in black was recovering now, using their suit's thrusters to stabilize and prepare for another approach. In the distance, I could see two more shapes emerging from a service hatch—reinforcements coming to stop whatever Jelini was doing.

"Probably a security team," Eggi said, sealing his helmet. "They must have spotted her. She's going to be in big trouble if they catch her."

I'd made my choice. I pushed off from the hull, and the others followed closely behind, using our suits' maneuvering thrusters to propel ourselves toward Jelini's position. The artificial gravity field weakened dramatically as we moved away from the ship's main hull, and I felt that familiar floating sensation in my stomach.

Construction equipment crowded the maintenance gantry—more coils of cable, partially assembled ducting segments, and other equipment floating on safety tethers keeping it from drifting away. The artificial gravity was fluctuating wildly here at the edge of the pressurized zone, and it made every movement a calculated risk.

"Jelini, what the hell do you think you're doing?" Jim's voice crackled over the comm channel.

She didn't respond, and continued to work frantically at the buoy's control panel. As we drew closer, I could see warning lights pulsing along the buoy's surface—red indicators that suggested something was very wrong.

"The core temperature readings are off the charts," Eggi said, his suit's sensors scanning the buoy. "Whatever she's doing is overloading the system."

Just as we were about to reach her, two more figures in sleek, black environmental suits emerged from a service hatch to our left. Even through the tinted faceplates, I recognized Mudar's sharp features in one suit, and Crasp's bulky frame in the other. It wasn't a security team at all.

"Stop them!" Mudar's voice boomed over an open channel. "The girl is tampering with a classified communications array!"

Crasp fired something from a tube mounted on his arm —not a projectile but some kind of magnetic restraint that nearly caught Jim's ankle, but he dodged just in time.

"Jelini!" I called, finally close enough to grab onto the maintenance scaffolding near the buoy. "Whatever you're doing, we need to go now!"

"I've almost got it, Mott!"

I realized I needed to do something to draw their attention away from Jelini. She wasn't going to give up, and the most immediate problem wasn't that she was at risk—it was that people were trying to apprehend her. If anyone from security was listening on the open channel, they would soon join the fray. We needed to divert them, make them see that she wasn't the person they should be pursuing.

But how?

"Eggi, Jim—on my mark, activate your emergency beacons," I whispered.

Jim gave me a questioning look, but Eggi caught on immediately. "We'll head in opposite directions. They'll have to split their forces."

"What about you?" Jim asked.

"I'll give them something even more interesting to chase."

Without waiting for their response, something caught my eye and I knew the time was now or never. I twisted my thruster controls to maximum and launched myself directly toward Mudar, an insane gambit that made him momentarily freeze in surprise. As I rocketed past him, I snagged a small device from his utility belt— what looked like an access key or command module. It may have been nothing special, but what mattered most was the idea it gave me.

I gesticulated wildly and waved the device in my hand. "I have override access to the royal fleet's security systems and I'm going to shut this entire ship down unless you come and get me!" I shouted over the open channel, hoping every security officer in range could hear me.

The reaction came fast. Mudar's attention snapped away from Jelini, his face contorting with rage. "After her!" he commanded, and two of his associates peeled away from Jelini's position to pursue me instead.

"Now!" I called to Jim and Eggi, and they activated their emergency beacons.

As I twisted through the construction debris, leading my pursuers on a wild chase, I caught a glimpse of Jelini still working at the buoy's control panel. Whatever she was doing there, at least now she had the time to finish it.

Mudar was closing in fast, his suit's thrusters clearly more powerful than our emergency models. Crasp swung around, trying to flank us.

Eggi was already moving, and as he moved, he cleared a path for us through the floating construction debris. Behind us, I could hear Crasp shouting orders into his comm as he pursued.

A bright flash of light burst from the buoy.

"She did it!" Jim's voice crackled over the comm. "Whatever she was trying to do—look!"

Through my faceplate, I watched as Jelini pushed away from the buoy, her maneuvering thrusters flaring as she propelled herself toward a nearby service hatch.

"I'm clear!" her voice called over the comm. "It can't be stopped now."

"Captain Mott, I've found an access point on the eastern quadrant," Eggi reported, his breathing heavy. "Security's responding to multiple alerts—they're spread thin."

"Same here," Jim added. "Western maintenance lock is practically unguarded. Everyone's focused on whatever Jelini just triggered."

I assessed our situation, acutely aware that my ragtag band of young clones were scattered across the exterior of the PNO with no coordinated escape plan.

"Let's meet at the central hub," I decided.

"The central hub?" Jim's voice carried clear concern. "That's where all the security checkpoints are!"

"It's also where all the access hatches are," I explained. "Which makes it the easiest place to catch transit out of here."

I tapped commands into my suit's interface and sent coordinates to everyone. "I'm flagging our rendezvous point on the shared map."

As the map deployed across our HUDs, I couldn't help wishing we'd aligned on this system before docking. Too late for regrets now—we had to move.

"Everyone copy?" I asked.

Three acknowledgments came through, including Jelini's excited "On my way!"

"Good. Stay in your suits until the last possible moment—they'll mask our identities. Central hub, ten minutes."

Jim, Eggi and I reached the airlock just as the buoy's warning lights shifted to a steady, brilliant white. Through my helmet, I could feel the vibrations as something inside the buoy began to breach.

The three of us tumbled into the airlock, the door sealing behind us as Crasp reached it. His fist pounded uselessly against the reinforced porthole.

As the chamber pressurized, we could feel the dull thud of an impact outside—not an explosion, but something stranger. Through the small porthole, I caught a glimpse of the buoy collapsing in on itself, creating a brief, brilliant flare before disappearing entirely.

"What was that?" Jim gasped, yanking off his helmet as soon as the pressure equalized.

"Implosion," Eggi said, his face pale. "The core compressed rather than exploded." He shook his head. "Very strange construction for a comm buoy."

"Jelini seems to be headed toward the port at the far end," I said, gesturing in that direction. "If we cut through a few rooms, we should be able to make sure she gets inside safe."

Alarms began blaring throughout the section as we shed our suits and raced into the corridor.

FLUX AND FALLOUT

We contemplate whether the royals had deposited us in a future where we would never catch up.

We ran through a series of administrative chambers, each one filled with important-looking people in formal attire. None of them gave any indication whatsoever of being the slightest bit aware, let alone concerned about, the mayhem we had just escaped. One room was hosting the most earnestly boring discussion ever imaginable about proper protocol for logging archived mining data.

"Furthermore," a particularly austere-looking official was saying, "the beta-phase formations must be labeled and flagged according to the standard seventeen-point reference system, not the simplified twelve-point scale that some of our younger data repositists have begun—"

That's when we crashed through their door, Jim tripping over his own feet and sprawling across their holoprojector table, scattering carefully arranged files and samples everywhere.

"Sorry!" I called out as we continued running. "Maintenance... drill, uh—training! Sir! Have a good recday!"

"This is exactly why we need stricter protocols!" I heard the official shout after us.

We rounded another corner but found our path blocked by a security checkpoint. With no Jelini in sight, we ducked into a side corridor, hoping to find another way around.

Just then, my comm unit buzzed with an incoming message—text only, no audio. It was from Jelini: "Central Assembly Chamber. HURRY. They're here."

"I said central hub, not the assembly chamber!" I repeated in disbelief. "That's where the Alphas are meeting with the royals!"

"What's she thinking?" Jim groaned. "She's going to get us all in so much trouble!"

Following emergency signage, we made our way toward the heart of the PNO. Behind us, I could hear the pounding of boots—security was on high alert, and Mudar and Crasp had surely made it back inside.

We burst through a final set of doors and found ourselves in the central assembly chamber to find chaos had already erupted. The massive room was filled with hundreds of dignitaries—the Alphas, their royal counterparts, and dozens of administrative officials.

At the far corner of the room, security guards were converging. I gestured to the others and we made our way there, ducking behind serving tables and coat racks and doing our best to avoid attracting too much attention to ourselves. Somewhere in the room were the Maltan elders.

After all we'd been through, being spotted by them would certainly bring a final and definitive end to our adventures.

The assembly chamber was a lush display of the royal fleet's finer resources—all crisp lines and ornate flourishes unlike anywhere on the IHC-111. High-ranking officials in formal attire mingled beneath crystal chandeliers. The air smelled of real food—not synthesized protein but actual grown delicacies from private hydroponic gardens—served by staff in starched uniforms.

Along one wall, a string quartet played music. The sound provided a genteel backdrop for conversations about policy and protocol in mission parameters.

Several ministers in ceremonial regalia huddled near a decorative fountain that cycled actual drinkable water just for show. Nearby, a cluster of royal engineers in formal uniforms adorned with merit badges discussed propulsion theories, and occasionally glanced toward the main doors with obvious apprehension.

At the center of it all stood a holographic display of star systems—our projected seeding paths rendered in detail.

As we drew closer to Jelini, the guards seemed confused about who to apprehend, Jelini, or Mudar and Crasp, who had just entered from another doorway, weapons drawn.

"Seize them!" Mudar shouted, spotting us. "They've destroyed vital equipment!"

The assembly chamber exploded with voices as Mudar advanced on us. The Alphas, along with Jelini and Jim's elders, rose from their seats at the far end of the room in confusion. Royal security guards moved to intercept, and to my relief, they were focused on Mudar and Crasp for the time being.

On our path to the exit door, we passed two engineering department heads locked in heated debate—one with an elaborate silver beard, the other with startlingly grey skin.

"The classification system is utterly inadequate!" the bearded man thundered, spittle flying from his lips. "We've been cataloging archives incorrectly for three generations!"

"Your proposed alternative would require recalibrating every scanner in the fleet," the other countered. "The resource expenditure alone—"

Their argument was cut short when a server carrying a tray of beverages, jostled by the room's growing commotion, stumbled between them. The drinks—deep burgundy cocktails in fluted glasses—splashed across both officials' formal attire.

Nearby, a young diplomat was discussing something with an older woman whose elaborate headpiece suggested either considerable rank or questionable style. Their hushed conversation continued despite the escalating chaos, and both glanced toward the sealed doors where royal security forces were gathering.

"Stand down immediately!" a security captain ordered from the room's corner, his weapon trained on Mudar.

"We need to get out of here," I muttered to the others. "Now."

Jelini had spotted us and was already making her way toward our position, ducking and dodging between confused officials. Before anyone could stop us, we slipped through a service door behind a decorative stand.

"The upper level!" Eggi shouted, pointing to a mezzanine overlooking the chamber. "There's another exit!"

We fought our way toward the spiral staircase leading up, while around us the assembly had devolved into complete chaos. Royal security and Crasp's men had begun exchanging fire, with officials diving under tables for cover.

The mezzanine gave temporary respite from the uproar. Through a series of small viewports, I could see that the area outside the assembly chamber was equally frantic, with more security personnel approaching, alarms flashing.

Jelini appeared from a side corridor, breathless and wide-eyed. "I did it!" she whispered triumphantly.

I grabbed her shoulders and gave her a huge hug. I didn't know what the hell she had been up to, but I was tremendously relieved to know that she was safe. "Jelini, *what* did you do?"

She looked at us each in turn. "I'm sorry for running off. But I couldn't just stand by. When I figured out what that buoy was programmed to do..." She took a deep breath and her eyes brightened.

"Did you see? It imploded! That's exactly what would happen if it was a dampening field!"

I checked the scans on my suit's display and frowned. "But Jelini, if that meant there was a ghost ship hiding somewhere, where is it now? I'm checking the whole sector and seeing only our same three ships. If something of any scale had been here recently, it would have left some sort of wake with its propulsion."

Her face fell. "It must be there," she insisted. "Why else would they all conspire together—the royals, Mudar, the renegade droids? It's like Smith says: 'Anytime enemies work together, you can be sure you're in for a fix.'"

She paused for a moment, clearly expecting accolades or some sort of praise.

"It was very spirited of you to do that, Jelini," I said gently, "but I'm afraid it doesn't pan out."

Whether Jelini had exposed a ghost ship or not, she'd certainly disrupted something important to some very powerful people.

Jim nodded. "We're going to be in big trouble if they find out we had something to do with this. What now?"

"Medical sector," I said firmly. "We find Beryl and get out of here."

Through a service corridor, we managed to make our way to a rapid transport junction—the PNO's internal shuttle system, used primarily by maintenance crews to quickly traverse the ship's vast sections. We piled into an empty transport pod just as the doors were closing.

The transport pod's gentle humming enveloped us in a cocoon of momentary safety. Had Mudar's gang really opened fire against a team of security personnel in a crowd full of Alphas and royals? I shuddered to think that we had managed to get tangled up in all this. I leaned my head against the cool metal wall and let the vibrations travel through my skull, grateful for these few minutes where no one was shooting at us, no one was trying to transform into mindless slaves, no one was chasing us through a field of asteroids.

Jim slumped beside me, his breathing gradually slowing to normal. The pod's dim lighting cast shadows across his face, the boy I'd been tasked with supervising now replaced by someone who had seen too much, too quickly.

Eggi sat cross-legged on the floor, clearly trying to account for all that we'd seen and encountered that night.

I closed my eyes, aware of every ache in my body, every bruise and strained muscle from our escape. The past hours felt dreamlike—had we really fought merchant droids, escaped a chop shop, and crashed a royal diplomatic gathering? Had I really almost fired weapons at Tam's ship out of pure hurt and rage? Was there really a massive conspiracy underway?

I wasn't the same person who had woken up this morning excited about a romantic getaway. That Mott seemed far away now.

The transport pod slowed as it approached the medical sector station. Through the viewport, I could see a group of some of Crasp's goons rushing past, unaware of our presence in the transport.

"Now's our chance," I said as the doors slid open. "Let's find Beryl and get out of this mess."

We moved quickly through the medical sector corridors. As we rounded a corner toward the isolation ward, a familiar figure stepped out from a service doorway— Hannick, looking uncharacteristically wary.

Gone was the confident swagger from our earlier encounter. Her posture was stooped, shoulders hunched and tense as if expecting trouble from any direction. Many of the pouches and pockets of her outfit had some flaps hanging open, and others bulged with stuff stashed there. This was not Hannick at her best. A thin sheen of sweat glistened on her forehead, and the former gleam in her eyes had been replaced by fatigue.

"There you are," she said, glancing over her shoulder. She seemed profoundly relieved to see us.

"What are you doing here?" I demanded.

"I was called in," she said with a shrug. "But seeing how things are deteriorating, I think a change of plans might be in order."

"You're working with them?" Jim accused.

Hannick's eyes narrowed. "I work with who pays." She gestured down the corridor. "What remains of Mudar's cohort is setting up shop in the east docking bay. But they apprehended him, which means that arrangement is no longer worth my while financially. And, well, what I didn't overhear from you all chattering in my cargo hold I learned from Rono," Hannick said. And just like that, she started to resemble her old self again. She leaned against the wall, picking casually at her tooth as if she had all the time in the world. "I tracked down your friend Beryl. Let me tell you, she is a real piece of work. She's entertaining, I'll grant that much." Her eyes narrowed with something that might have been respect. "Nearly took out two security officers with nothing but a medical scanner and a stolen sample container. By the time I found her, she was knee-deep in data cartridges and muttering about 'finally seeing the big picture.'"

"You want me to believe that you've turned heroic all of a sudden? Where is Beryl?" I asked.

"Your friend is fine," Hannick assured me. "She's smarter than she looks. She's waiting for us at my ship."

"Why the hell is she on your ship? I am not in the mood for any more shit, certainly not from the likes of you."

"Relax, relax," she said. "You know, it's not that hard for someone like me to dig up intel on people. Plan A was to apprehend her for Crasp to reel you all in together. But as I just told you, we're thoroughly into Plan B now. I'm not trying to squeeze you for anything, kid. I learned from a very young age that it's best to side with the person who's most likely to win. Right now, my money's on you. Beryl's safe, and she's free to go whenever she wants. You're lucky I found her when I did. You and your friends have a special knack for getting into trouble, and it took some smooth talking and a little bribery on my part to keep her from going to the PNO detainment center."Hannick smiled with narrowed eyes. "You're welcome," she said smugly. "Not everyone would risk their reputation helping a bunch of kids playing hero. Consider it professional courtesy... or maybe I just like backing the underdogs."

I didn't sense a lie, but I also didn't feel anything besides anger toward Hannick at the moment. As much as I wanted to believe everyone had a heart, the train of thought she'd just outlined painted the picture of a bloodless mercenary. I said nothing.

"Come on," she said. "You'll want to see this."

I looked to the others. Jim gave a grumpy shrug and Eggi nodded that we might as well go ahead and get this over with.

Following Hannick through a series of maintenance shortcuts, we arrived at an observation gallery overlooking the east docking bay. Below us, Mudar's remaining gang were gathered around a large metallic cube—approximately four meters on each side, with no obvious access points or controls.

"What is that thing?" Eggi whispered.

"Stasis cube," Hannick replied, her voice unusually serious. "Puts the occupant in a sort of suspended animation—sometimes for years."

"Stasis?" Jim repeated. "For what purpose?"

"In Mudar's case, it's part of a standing deal with the powers that be," Hannick said, lowering her voice. "Instead of standard judicial rigamarole, they honor an agreement. He gets put in this proprietary system for a while, goes into stasis, and supposedly comes out rehabilitated."

"That's scarily fast," I said. I couldn't have imagined the judicial system working so efficiently. Clearly this had been planned for, which, I supposed, meant there were teams of people in our society who had been plotting to get Mudar behind bars, and although that made me feel less alone, it didn't console me.

She tapped the holographic display to enlarge a section of the cube's readout. "The purpose is to expose the person inside to a cognitive reconditioning system called 'Constructive Dreaming,' ostensibly developed as rehab tech for deep trauma recovery. But for our friend here, it's going to be more like behavioral modification. They'll immerse him in elaborately crafted scenarios designed to stimulate creative problem-solving and empathy development."

"'Him?'"

"Somewhere in there, Mudar is—or was—a human."

My jaw dropped open.

"There's a lot you need to learn about the underbelly of our strange little society here, my young friend. Of course, you don't have to dig deeper. Most choose not to." She gestured toward a passing group of maintenance workers, their expressions more or less the same. "They stick to their training materials, do their scheduled tasks. Anything that doesn't fit—" She made a dismissive gesture, brushing invisible dust from her sleeve. "They simply... don't see it anymore. Probably easier that way, but personally, ignorance is not a gamble I'd be willing to take."

Hannick's wrist device flashed to life with a soft blue glow. She angled it toward us, the holographic display hovering inches above her skin depicting cross-sections of the stasis cube's internal mechanisms.

"See for yourself," she murmured, her finger tracing through the projection to expand certain elements.

I leaned closer, squinting. Lines of text scrolled past too quickly to read completely, but phrases like "immersive scenario generation" and "empathy module activation" caught my eye. The cube really was a psychological reconditioning system.

Jelini gasped beside me. "They're going to rewrite his mind."

"I wouldn't say 'rewrite,'" Hannick said, her eyes never leaving the display. "More like... continuous therapy without the option to walk out." Her finger swiped to reveal the program queue—thousands of simulations scheduled to run in sequence over years, each designed to break down and rebuild different aspects of consciousness.

On Hannick's screen, I could see the program queue scheduled for Mudar's multi-year rehabilitation:

"Human and Mechanical Empathy Training" - simulations where he would experience existence from the perspective of countless humans and machines, feeling their functionality, limitations, and interdependence with other systems.

"Collaborative Design Studios" - endless workshops where he would conceptualize new technologies but could only implement them through consensus-building with simulated personalities programmed to challenge his assumptions.

Each program seemed unappetizing. But as a continuous, unrelenting experience with no ability to withdraw consent or rest between sessions? The thought of being trapped in a loop of enforced creativity and emotional processing was its own kind of horror.

I began to contemplate the darkness of this "standing agreement." Who monitored the process? Who decided when Mudar was "fixed" enough to rejoin society?

"This is considered humane?" I whispered to Hannick.

She shrugged, eyes never leaving the control panel as it cycled through initialization. "Compared to what? At least this way he gets to keep existing, after a fashion."

But I couldn't shake the creeping dread. If the governing body could rewrite someone's mind with their "Constructive Dreaming," what stopped them from replacing rehabilitation with something worse? From erasing inconvenient personalities and implanting compliant ones?

Hannick led us down to the bay level through a service elevator. As we approached, I could see Mudar standing before the stasis cube. Next to him was a royal scientist, judging by the uniform, making adjustments to a control panel that had extended from the cube's surface.

The chamber hummed to life, its neural interfaces connecting with Mudar's altered biology. His eyes widened in momentary panic before the sedation protocols took effect.

"Consider that my resignation," Hannick said to Mudar's unconscious form.

I watched a man disappear into the machine, knowing whoever emerged years later would technically have his face, but nothing else might remain.

The feeling came at me sideways, like something broken loose in the ship's ventilation—a wrong pressure, a metal taste. Seeing how different our society was from what I'd been trained on made my chest feel scraped out and strange, like I'd been breathing recycled air my whole life without knowing it.

She turned to us, her expression unreadable. "We should go."

"The renegades," Jelini said as we hurried toward Hannick's ship, "they're not actually trying to take over the seeders, are they? They're trying to change what it means to be human."

"They think they are," Hannick replied. "But I've seen too many would-be perfecters of humanity come and go. In the end, it's always the messy, unoptimized biological humans who survive. Despite all odds."

She led us through a final security checkpoint and flashed a badge that made the guards step aside without question. We followed her into a small briefing room adjacent to her docking bay.

"I'm guessing you realize that the communications buoy you sabotaged wasn't just a buoy," Hannick continued, her voice dropping lower. "It was part of a network designed to obscure something very important to a few of the royals."

Jelini crossed her hands in front of her chest and narrowed her eyes at me. She was gloating.

"Like a top-secret project or something?"

"All I know is that some key royals made a deal with certain droid collectives. The droids provide security, enforcement, and specialized labor for this program they call Flux. In exchange, they get something they've wanted for a long time—recognition as a sovereign species with their own dedicated territories on these new worlds."

Eggi frowned. "But why would the royals share power with the droids?"

"I don't think they're sharing power as much as appointing droids to do their jobs for them while they gallivant on whatever this Flux project is all about," Hannick said simply. "So that's what Mudar and Crasp were betting on," I said. "They were security contractors, and if everything went right, they would be handsomely rewarded with official power."

"Was it a ghost ship?"

"We should be so lucky." Hannick made a sound like metal scraping against rock. "No. Ghost ships—those are just the fairy stories people tell themselves when they need to explain their fear of being alone in a tin can in a sea of darkness. I don't think disabling that buoy will have an effect on the bigger agenda, but circumstances have certainly gotten mucked up for Mudar and Crasp, at least."

She checked her wrist device. "Time for you to head out. Your friend is waiting."

THE EXTRACTION

Reunions should feel triumphant. Ours, we didn't know what to do with yet.

Through the Maltan shuttle's viewport, we watched the royal fleet's medical sector recede behind us when Beryl suddenly grabbed my arm.

"There!" she pointed to something faint from behind one of the station's massive radiator arrays. "That's what I saw earlier!"

I saw nothing. Then—a brief flicker, like reflected light caught on something that shouldn't be there, and a faint trail of luminescence. Not the familiar exhaust pattern of any drive system I'd ever seen.

"Do you see it?" Beryl's voice quavered, her eyes wide and unblinking. "Tell me you see it too."

It was a shimmer, nothing more. But of what? Not debris. Something solid emitting no light, trailing an impossibly faint wake.

"It's a ship," Beryl whispered, her breath fogging the viewport. "With faster-than-light capability. I know it. All this time, I knew someone had cracked the barrier."

I leaned forward, squinting at the ghostly outline. "No, look at the hull configuration. Those are IHC maintenance markers." The faint structural lines matched our own ship's design.

"That's not possible," Jim said. "The IHC is..." He turned to check our position readings. "The IHC is way over portside."

"Maybe it's a reflection?" I suggested. "Some kind of optical phenomenon?"

Eggi was pouring through sensor readings. "I'm not really picking anything up on any of these scans."

The vessel—if it was a vessel—seemed to fold in on itself, the familiar lines of an IHC maintenance dock waving like a curtain before disappearing entirely.

"Did you see that?" Jelini breathed. "It was like... like space ate it."

I felt a strange sensation in my chest. For just a moment, I'd felt something familiar.

"It could be a temporal echo," Beryl said slowly. "The ship casting shadows through time. That would explain why it looks like the IHC but appears in the wrong place."

"Or a probability ghost," Eggi added. "A ship that exists in quantum superposition—neither fully there nor not there."

But I shook my head, remembering that strange feeling of recognition. "Space seemed to bend around it," I traced the motion with my hand. "Could it be space was being... pinched?"

We stared at the empty space where the phenomenon had been. The silence that followed felt heavy.

"Whatever it is," I said finally, "it's more than just a legend or fairy tale."

"But if it's not faster-than-light travel..." Beryl trailed off.

"Think about it," Eggi said. "What if they could fold space, create connections between distant points? They could step through, go anywhere instantly."

"Or bring things here," Jim added darkly.

"We need to find out what's on the other side," Beryl said firmly. "I think it's got everything to do with your ReGenesis program."

"Hey, don't call it mine. But, what do you mean?"

"What if they've already identified several promising planets? What if they're using this technology to establish direct colonies there rather than just seeding life and letting it evolve naturally?"

"While the rest of us continue our endless journey," Eggi added bitterly.

Beryl's face was grim. "It's probably worse than that. If ReGenesis was creating a new type of human, that means they're hatching something else in preparation for life on these new worlds."

"What do you mean?" Jim asked.

"I don't know. Who knows what the real effects of flux might be? But you said you learned that at least some among the royal actually want to engineer obedient quasi-mechanical human life forms."

"That would leave the droids to stay behind to govern everyone left behind," Jim added.

"If they have that kind of technology, why not just... take over?" I asked.

"Because they need us," Beryl said simply. "The maintenance workers, everyone aboard the three ships—we're their support system while they perfect the technology. Until they don't need us anymore."

No one answered. Outside, the stars continued their cold, distant vigil. Inside our small craft, we considered a universe suddenly much larger and stranger than we'd been taught to believe.

Beryl's hand slipped from my arm, leaving ghost-impressions of her fingers. She'd been gripping me for support this whole time. "Then again, maybe it was nothing," she murmured, but her eyes never left the viewport. "Space plays tricks on tired eyes. We're young and full of partial facts gleaned from a few brief scans of data that was stolen from crime lords and sleazeballs. Besides, I am, after all, a well-known conspiracy theorist with anxiety issues. This wouldn't be the first time I thought I'd made sense of things."

"No," I said firmly. "We may not know everything, but we have learned enough to suspect that at least some among the royals are intending to betray everything the seeder mission stands for."

"What can we possibly do about it?" Eggi asked. "They're the royals. They control everything."

I thought about Tooch, about the community we'd glimpsed at the School of Ore. About Rono and Hannick and all the others who carved out their own existence at the edges of the official society.

"Not everything," I said. "And they only control what we let them control. This information we uncovered needs to be shared. Not just aboard the IHC, but everywhere in the fleet."

"They'll just deny it," Jim said.

"We have tons of incriminating evidence." I looked squarely at Jim. "And we might be able to get more. I'm sure we're not alone in this."

I wanted it to be true. Whatever was coming, whatever changes the royal fleet was planning, I didn't want us to be the only players in this game.

"We have evidence," Jim said. "But we have no power."

"So we just give up?" Beryl demanded. "Let them win?"

"We stay safe," Jim said firmly. "We forget what we saw. We go back to our lives."

"That's assuming they let us," Eggi said quietly. "That's assuming no one comes after us."

The room went quiet.

"Mott," Beryl said carefully. "What are you thinking?"

What was I thinking? That Jim was right—we were outmatched. Eggi was right, too. What we'd done today had put a target on our backs.

I thought about my parents. About all the maintenance workers and miners and service crew who lived and died following rules made by people who saw them as expendable.

I thought about Tam, and how I'd spent my whole life making myself small, quiet, helpful.

I thought about the woman I'd been this morning—counting stars and waiting for permission to matter.

"Here's what I'm thinking," I said slowly. "We're not ready. We have no allies, no plan, no power."

Jim looked relieved. Jelini looked devastated.

"But pretending we never saw anything—that's choosing to be part of the machine that grinds us down."

"So what do you suggest?" Beryl asked.

"We build something," I said. "We find others who've seen the cracks in the system. Others who are tired of being told their lives don't matter. We organize. We learn. We prepare."

"That's too risky," Jim protested, rubbing his fist. "You saw with Tam how hard it is to know who you can trust."

"You're asking us to commit to this," Beryl said. "Long term. To risk everything, maybe for nothing."

"I'm not asking," I corrected. "I'm saying what I'm going to do. You can all walk away. I won't blame you. I won't think less of you." I looked at each of them. "But if you stay, you're committing to the long game."

Silence.

I was a maintenance worker with mediocre grades and no special status. Just hours ago, I'd nearly gotten us all caught with a rookie mistake.

"I've spent my whole life learning how to fix things, and we've just come across something big that needs to be fixed. I'm not going to just hope someone else takes care of it."

Jim studied me for a long moment. Then, slowly, he nodded.

"I'm in," Beryl said, moving to stand beside me. "You're right. About all of it."

"Me too," Eggi added.

Jelini was the last to speak. "This is insane. We're going to regret this." She smiled grimly. "I'm in."

I felt the weight of their trust settle onto my shoulders. It was the most real thing I'd ever felt.

CONSPIRATORS AND COMRADES

We discuss the future of humanity and turn "proper pro-cedures" into an inside joke.

Back in the familiar corridors of the IHC-111, we were all trying to process everything we'd seen when my cabin's comm system chimed with an incoming transmission. The Alphas' formal identification code flashed on the screen. We all froze.

I hit the accept button, trying to compose my features into something resembling normal exhaustion rather than post-adventure adrenaline crash. Gelda and Lemoy Maltan's faces appeared, their expressions more or less conveying the same authority and composure as earlier that day.

"Ah, Mott," Gelda said, smiling serenely. "I trust our young ones haven't been too much trouble?"

Behind me, Jim and Jelini tried to look as innocent as possible while Beryl attempted to become one with the shadows in the corner. Eggi had already slipped into my maintenance closet.

"Not at all," I replied, perhaps too quickly. "It was a... reasonably educational day."

"Indeed," Lemoy nodded. "We've just concluded a rather eventful meeting ourselves. The future of seeder operations even became a topic of discussion."

"I imagine the security breach made things particularly interesting," I said without thinking, then immediately wished I could snatch the words back.

Both Alphas' expressions sharpened. "Security breach?" Gelda asked carefully.

"Oh, uh, we heard the alarms— I mean— we heard *about* the alarms," I stumbled to recover. "From here. In my cabin. Where we've been. The whole time."

"Ah yes," Lemoy's eyes narrowed slightly. "I believe there may have been a minor issue with the environmental systems. Nothing to concern yourselves with."

I caught Jelini starting to open her mouth, probably to correct their assumption, and quickly spoke over her. "Well, you know what they say about environmental systems. Always cycling through their processes!"

There was an awkward pause where I tried not to look like someone who had recently been in a zero-gravity fight with cyborg conspirators.

"Right," Gelda said finally. "Well, we'll be sending someone shortly to escort Jim and Jelini back to their ward. I trust they're packed and ready?"

"Absolutely," I nodded enthusiastically. "They're already ready already. They learned so much today about... proper procedures and... protocol following."

Behind me, I heard Beryl stifle what might have been a laugh or a groan.

"Excellent," Lemoy said, his eyes glazed over with a familiar boredom. "You have our appreciation. May your next week at work be a productive one."

The transmission ended and we all let out a collective breath.

"Proper procedures and protocol following?" Beryl emerged from her corner, grinning. "Smooth."

"Hey, you try making casual conversation with the Alphas right after discovering the royal fleet is trying to transcend human evolution," I shot back.

"At least they bought it," Jim said.

"Right," I said. "Eggi? You can come out of the locker now."

"I think I fell asleep there for a second," his muffled voice replied. "It's surprisingly peaceful back on this ship."

Sometimes I wondered if the Maltans knew more than they let on. If they remembered their own youthful adventures and chose to look the other way. Could they really be so self-absorbed that they hadn't noticed anything? I had to bet on it.

"I've been thinking about that word," Jelini said suddenly, breaking the contemplative silence that had fallen over us. "Flux."

We all turned to her, gathered around my small cabin table where various pieces of evidence lay scattered.

"What if it's not just faster-than-light technology?" she continued, her fingers tracing patterns on the tabletop. She shrugged. "Anyway, it's a perfect name for what's happening to all of us."

Jim leaned forward. "What do you mean?"

"Flux,'" I said, testing the words. "That's what they're really creating. On one level, it's literal—using flux drive technology to colonize planets, bypass generations of waiting."

Jim nodded approvingly. "But flux also means transition, uncertainty..."

"Exactly!" Jelini's eyes lit up. "Our entire mission is in flux now. Everything we thought we knew about what it means to be seeders, about our purpose—it's all changing."

I felt something click into place. "The royals and those like Mudar and Crasp are betting on a future where they control who gets to move between worlds, while the rest of us continue our journey, unaware that everything has changed."

I looked at each of them in turn—these unlikely companions brought together by circumstance.

"We need a name," I said decisively. "If we're going to resist this, to make sure this technology benefits everyone, not just the elite, we need to organize."

"Starseed," Jelini suggested. "Obviously."

We waited for her to elaborate further.

"We all descended from the seeders, whether we're royal or not. Like the Smith line about tending the garden or whatever: 'Before the royal fleet there were the outcasts, before the outcasts the dreamers, and before the dreamers

240

only stars.' We're all the same, and we want to uncover the truth of our mission."

"A movement dedicated to ensuring that the future of humanity isn't decided by a privileged few," Jim added.

I nodded, and a strange calm settled over me. Maybe this was what real responsibility felt like—choosing to stand for something greater than yourself.

"Starseed it is," I agreed. "Hopefully we'll find others we can trust who hold the same vision." I glanced at the clock. "As for our first mission, Operation 'This Was Definitely A Normal Day' begins now," I announced, surveying the chaos in my cabin. "Jim, Jelini, you've been studying maintenance protocols. Beryl, we need to get you out of here before anyone starts asking why you're not at your post."

We moved with the efficiency of a well-drilled maintenance crew, which, I supposed, we had actually become through this adventure. Beryl gathered her scanner and the various pieces of evidence she'd collected, and paused only to give each of us a quick, fierce hug before slipping out through my cabin's secondary access panel.

Just as we finished stashing away the last evidence of our adventure, a sharp knock at the door announced the arrival of the Maltan messenger, a junior diplomatic aide whose crisp uniform and perfectly regulation haircut made my cabin look even more shabby by comparison.

"I'm here to escort the young clones back to their quarters," he announced, managing to convey with just his tone how beneath his station this duty was.

Jim and Jelini gathered their things—actual study materials we'd hastily arranged on my workbench.

"Thank you for an... educational evening, Mott," Jelini said.

"Indeed," Jim added. "We learned so much about... proper procedures."

"I'm grateful to have been given this opportunity to rise to the occasion of performing supervision duties," I told them, loud enough for the aide to hear. "And now it's time to focus on my prescribed maintenance work."

The aide nodded with bored approval.

I closed the door and looked around my pristine cabin. Everything was back to regulation standard. But we'd seen behind the curtain of our society.

BETWEEN SYSTEMS AND STARS

In which Tooch returns with a resonance amplifier and I realize some stories are just beginning.

I had just settled into my favorite repair chair with a steaming cup of chocomellow, a rare luxury I'd been saving for a special occasion—and surviving this day certainly qualified as that—when my door chimed again. For a moment, I tensed, expecting an official inquiry, but the figure in my doorway was Tooch Shawno.

He held something in his hands. I recognized Jelini's portable resonance amplifier. She must have dropped it at some point during one of our many hasty exits. The small device caught the cabin's light and sent tiny rainbows dancing across the walls.

"Thought someone might want this back," he said, trying and failing to sound casual. "Though honestly, I'm more interested in something else I heard about. A certain maintenance worker with plans to explore the outer reaches? Maybe set up an independent operation?"

I felt my face flush. "That was... before I understood what was really out there." Images of the mysterious ship, of Mudar in the stasis pod, of everything we'd seen today flashed through my mind.

"Ah," he nodded, stepping into my cabin and examining my tool collection with genuine interest. "Saw something that changed your perspective?"

"Several somethings," I admitted, setting the resonance amplifier carefully on my workbench, "And you know, there might be a better way. Between total independence and blind loyalty to the system."

"Interesting modification," Tooch said, examining my comm system. "Subspace-murmur's usually restricted to emergency channels."

"I'm full of surprises," I replied, then felt my face flush again at how that sounded.

But Tooch just smiled—that genuine, unguarded smile that had first caught my attention at the party. "I'm counting on it," he said softly.

Outside my viewport, the eternal starfield wheeled slowly past. Somewhere out there, that mysterious ship was probably still moving through space in ways we couldn't understand. The royal fleet was plotting their transformation of humanity. And we—this strange group of friends brought together by chance and adventure—would plan our resistance.

ABOUT THE AUTHOR

Stephen Lloyd Webber lives in Austin, Texas.

For updates on upcoming books and events, visit:
stephenlloydwebber.com and tmmw.io